BAI

Marlene's not like the other humans. They weep while she smiles. They look at us with fear, while she entices me with a come-hither look.

I...have no idea why such a bold female resonated to a male like me. I am the most reticent of all the sa-khui tribe, a hunter that never expected to have a family of my own. But resonance chooses, and it has chosen her for me. And Marlene is quite determined to seduce me...and who can say no to such a woman?

This story explores the long-awaited romance of Marlene and Zennek. Even though it is a 'flashback' to the beginning of the Ice Planet Barbarians series, it can be read out of order. Enjoy!

BARBARIAN'S SEDUCTION

ICE PLANET BARBARIANS BOOK 20 - A SCIFI ALIEN ROMANCE

RUBY DIXON

WWW.RUBYDIXON.COM

1

MARLENE

*E*ven though it has been more than twelve years since *Maman* passed away, I see signs of her everywhere. *Maman* is in the endless white snow, because she loved a good snowfall. She is in the crisp, fresh air because she adored a morning walk with her daughter, just like I am doing with mine. Most of all, though, she is in Zalene's goofy little giggles as she hops between one cobblestone to the next. Sometimes I think my little daughter is all Zennek, with her thick body and flashing tail, her quiet moods and easy smile...but then she will giggle over the most absurd things and I am reminded of how my *Maman* loved to laugh.

"*Fais attention, ma petite cocotte*," I caution my daughter as her boots skid on the cobblestones. Even though she has sprouted up in this last year, I still call her babyish things like *cocotte* and *chou-*

chou because she's always going to be my little baby. There have been no more kits for me and my Zennek as of yet, but I don't really mind. I like my small family. When another resonance strikes us, it will be grand, but until then I will focus on my little Zalene. I want to be as close to her as I was with *ma mère*.

Of course, my father was not in my life, and so it was only me and my mother. That is not the case with my little Zalene, and so I must share her with Zennek. This day will be one of those "shared" days. Zalene and I take our morning walk, and then she will be going with her father to check traps this afternoon. That is another way my daughter takes after her strong, handsome, silent father—she loves to hunt. I do not have the stomach for it, but oh, my Zalene is a bloodthirsty one. She brought down her first hopper just last season and talks all the time of when she will be old enough to hunt dvisti with her father.

Zalene springs ahead of me, then dances back, all wiggling child-ishness. "What are you thinking about, *Maman*?"

I smile at her and hold out my hand as we walk to the dirtbeak nests. We don't need fuel, but I have my gathering basket and we're going to check for eggs. It's mostly just an excuse so we can have our precious mother-daughter time together before the day starts. "I was thinking about your *grand-mère*. She loved the snow."

Zalene lets go of my hand and races forward again, noticing a particularly deep drift of snow piled against the side of one of the high walls that encase the village. She flings herself into it, snow flying around her in a puff, and then flops onto her back and windmills her arms and legs. "She should have come with you, *Maman*! There is so much snow here!"

My heart aches, but I smile, rolling my eyes at my daughter's nonstop energy. "*Grand-mère* is in heaven. I told you this. She is gone."

"But you always say she is with you."

"She is with me," I agree, and tap my chest. "In my heart, but her spirit watches over me, *coco*." I move to my daughter's side and take her hand, helping her up from the snow bank she's destroyed. I crouch and dust snow off of her leathers, even though it's a futile gesture. In five minutes, she will be completely covered once again. "She sends me little signs to let me know all is well."

"Like the hearts?" Zalene asks before prancing away again.

"*Oui*, the hearts."

It's something I've only talked about with Zennek and my daughter, because most of the women I am stranded with are very practical. They have families they left behind back on Earth—or some, like Josie, had no family at all. But growing up it was always Marlene *et* Cecile, daughter and mother, and we were so close that when she died of cancer, I felt as if my world ended. Before she passed, *Maman* told me she would always watch over me. That she would give me signs.

That was when I started to see the hearts.

Maman loved hearts, and Valentine's Day, *et l'amour*. She was a romantic, a dreamer, and too good for the world. The day after she passed, I saw a bright red balloon in the shape of a heart float past in the sky. It made me think of her. At her funeral, the leaves that fell to the ground were heart-shaped. After that, I began to see hearts everywhere. They would flash up on a screen, or someone would stamp one to a receipt. There would be heart-shaped cookies at my favorite bakery. I would see them everywhere, and I knew it was *Maman* reminding me that we were still together, always.

Even after coming here, I see them. I see them in the stars at night, or in the pattern of leaves in my tea. I see them pressed into the snow, or a cloud that is shaped like a heart. Even on another planet, *Maman* watches over her Marlene. I scan the ground around me, looking for such signs, for her to let me know that all is well yet again today. The hearts are comforting, a silent hello from a loved one I can no longer hug.

"Ew!"

I'm drawn from my thoughts as Zalene makes a gagging noise. "What is it?"

She lifts her foot and shakes her little fur boot. "I stepped in poop!"

"Which foot?" I ask immediately, going to her side.

"The dirty one!" She gives me a dramatic look that would otherwise make me laugh, but I can't help but frown as I realize it's her right foot. *Maman* was always very superstitious, and I am the same. Stepping in animal droppings is good luck...but only for the left foot. For the right, it is not good. I do not say this to my daughter, though, because she is still young enough that such things upset her. "Did you make a heart out of it?"

Zalene studies the squished turd in the snow. "No. It's just a big flat circle of old poop." She leans over it, full if childlike fascination as she holds her nose. "Do you think it was Chompy's? Or Mr. Fluffypuff? Should we pick it up so we can burn it?"

"*Mais non*," I say immediately, hurrying her along. "Leave it be. We will get nests for fuel when we need to. We do not gather all the poop, *coco*." And I try not to think about it. It's nothing, just me being superstitious. I look for a sign from my mother that she agrees, but there are no hearts today from what I can see. Just snow.

It is nothing. Nothing at all.

WE RETURN from our morning walk and my mate Zennek is waiting at the front of our hut for our return. He scoops Zalene into his big arms and tweaks one of her fat, short little braids. He says nothing in greeting, letting his smile speak for him. My quiet, handsome mate. Just seeing his broad face makes the unease in my heart lessen.

I am worrying over nothing. It was merely my daughter stepping in animal dung on a path that often has animal dung. I move forward and kiss my mate's cheeks in greeting, even though I but crawled from his embrace a short time ago. I just like seeing him blush, and even after all this time, he still colors at the base of his horns, as if a kiss on each cheek is scandalous and full of lust.

For me it is, of course, but I am always full of lust when it comes to him. "My handsome mate," I purr, sliding a hand to his waist and then caressing his backside and the base of his tail. "Do you leave me soon?"

"Soon," he agrees, and sets Zalene down and points. "Go inside and put on your heavy boots." She scurries in and the moment she is out of sight, Zennek pulls me close and presses a kiss to my mouth. "We will not stay out long."

"Not if you want your tail pulled again," I agree, teasing. He is not quite as shy as the day I met him, but it has always been clear that I am the bold one. I don't mind this. It's fun, and it makes his occasional boldness that much more exciting. I enjoy his embrace, loving that he stoops low enough to nuzzle my nose and places another kiss on my lips. He breathes in my scent and I burrow against his warmth, happy.

"Strong weather above," he murmurs, fingers tracing my jaw. "Need more fuel?"

"We have plenty," I tell him, but his comment reminds me that this is *la saison brutale* and Zalene had an unlucky step this morning. I straighten his thick, furry tunic, fussing over him as he reluctantly lets me go. "You will stay warm? Be safe? Watch your steps?" He nods and I continue. "Should you leave Zalene?"

"It is fine."

I bite back a sigh. I know he loves his papa-daughter hunts as much as Zalene does. Soon she will be big enough to carry a real spear and then I will truly worry. "I saw a bad omen this morning. Mind yourselves."

"Your mother?" he asks. He knows I look for little signs of her "spirit" being nearby. When I shake my head and cast him a worried look, he leans in and nuzzles my face again. "I will be most careful."

"Watch Zalene closely," I ask.

He nods, and then our daughter flings herself at our waists, all childish glee. "We ready to go, Papa?"

"Ready," he says, and pulls her tiny bone spear from his backpack. He has made her miniature copies of his own gear, and I love how close they are. My heart tightens in my chest as I smile and wave, watching them go toward the pulley, hand in hand, spears at the ready.

These days are good, I remind myself. It is bonding time for them. If my father had not abandoned my mother when I was three, would I not have wanted the same thing?

I am just worrying for the sake of worrying. I look around at my surroundings, hoping for a small sign from my mother, but there is nothing. Even inside, I scan the discarded laundry and blankets, hoping for a symbol in the shape of a heart, but I see nothing but wrinkles. Frustrated, I straighten things up and then, since I have the day to myself, I head over to visit Zennek's *mére et pére*.

Kemli and Borran are just waking as I shake the bone chimes I made for them. "*Coucou*," I call out in greeting, then wait for the screen to be moved and for me to be invited in.

"Enter," Borran calls out, and I push inside, replacing the screen before much cold air can get inside. I'm not entirely surprised to see old Vadren piling out of their furs. It happens from time to time—Vadren has no kits or mate of his own, and Kemli and Borran's children have all mated and have families. Their youngest, Farli, mated recently and is at the Icehome beach, so Kemli and Borran have found themselves with too much hut and not enough heads to look after. At first I told myself that Vadren simply joined them for body heat and company, but Zennek just blushed and admitted that Vadren and Kemli were pleasure-mates before she resonated to Borran, and perhaps they are all three pleasure-mates again.

La. I cannot judge. They are adults. They are happy, and I am happy for them. I enter with a brilliant smile and kiss cheeks—including Vadren's—and then move toward the kitchen area. "Can I make you all tea? *Petit-déjeuner*?"

"Oh, daughter, let me," Kemli says, but I cluck fiercely at her until she sits down once more. They are elderly and I know their bones hurt in the brutal season, so I like to come and help out.

"Back under the covers with all three of you," I say, picking up a bone utensil from Kemli's stone countertop and waving it at them. "You can come out when the place is warm and your bellies are full."

They chuckle at my bossiness, but I know they like it. I keep up a steady stream of chatter, telling them all about Zalene and our walk this morning, and what Zennek is up to as I put on a morning stew and steep a pouch of tea. Farli looked after them when she lived at home, but now that she is gone to Icehome, Tiffany, Stacy and I make sure that they are taken care of and their fuel baskets are always overflowing and there are leftovers to warm up. Kemli loves to cook and fuss over people, but she also grows tired more quickly than before, so I don't mind stepping in. Zennek and I perhaps look after them more than the others, but we only have Zalene to fuss over. Tiffany has Lukti, but she also takes on all the plants in the village and a variety of other projects, whereas Stacy handles all of the central fire cooking while fussing over her young sons. I don't mind. Zennek has his parents and in a way, they are my parents, too. So I cook and I clean and I make them clothing to keep the cold away.

My heart skips a beat when I pull out her not-potatoes to chop for a stew. Kemli has them stored in a shallow basket, and the skins have been browned slightly so they can be chopped easier, a trick Stacy taught me. But the way they're laid out and lined up, they look just like loaves of bread that have been turned on their backs. Hastily, I flip them over and then cross myself, murmuring a quick prayer to the saints like my mother always did. Loaves on their back is bad luck.

These aren't loaves, but...this is the second bad sign. My fretting intensifies.

"I made Zalene coo-kees last night," Kemli says, walking up behind me. She's bundled in furs and picks through some of her baskets before setting one down triumphantly in front of me. "Her favorite."

I smile absently at Kemli and hug her close. Zalene indeed loves *Grand-mère* Kemli's cookies, especially the herbs-and-hraku mixture that is bafflingly awful to everyone but Zalene. My chubby little daughter probably doesn't need more cookies, but she's active and healthy, so I let her eat as much as she likes, even if Kemli is stuffing her like a piglet. "You are good to us," I tell Kemli, determined not to look at the not-potatoes.

Now I am just worrying myself.

I eat breakfast with the three elders and listen to them tell stories. I love hearing about my mate, how Zennek was always shy, how he would fight with Salukh and Pashov like angry snowcats, and the pranks they pulled as youngsters. The elders always have dozens of stories, and I normally enjoy sitting and relaxing the morning away with them, sewing in hand, but today I cannot seem to sit still. I'm antsy, and after I clean the dishes and store the rest of the stew in a bowl with a heavy lid and place it in the snow behind the hut to keep it cold, I throw back on my furs. "I promised Ariana I would sew with her today. Do you need anything?"

Borran gets to his feet and I can practically hear his bones creak. He looks how I imagine Zennek will when he is older, his dark hair streaked with silver and his face lined. His body is strong and thick like my mate's but shows the wear of time. "I have extra leathers I saved for you, daughter. Perhaps they will make a nice tunic for Zalene?"

Zalene already has a dozen tunics—both from my efforts and Kemli's—but I beam and take the leather, promising to make something pretty. With the cookies and roll of leather in my arms, I hurry out of there and head for Ariana's hut next door to mine. Of all of the women I am here with, Ariana is my closest friend. We are less social than the others, I think, so we lean on each other more and more. She struggles with her anxiety, and I so rarely worry over anything, so we are a good balance for each other. Today, however, I am the one full of worry and I want to talk to my friend. Perhaps speaking my fears aloud will make them disappear.

I scratch at Ariana's hut and wait for my friend, clutching the leather close to my chest. Her soft laughter floats through the air, followed by a baby's gurgle. A moment later, Zolaya comes to the entrance, his long hair freshly braided. He nods at me and lets me in, and as I duck inside, I see Ariana in her chair, her newborn at her breast as she nurses. I watch the little tiny tail flick as Zoari suckles, and feel a little stab of envy. I do not mind just one little *bébé*, but sometimes when I see *un petit enfant* I miss the sweet face and tiny, whirling tail as she nursed.

Analay is playing with carved toys in the middle of the floor, and Zolaya moves to his side and helps him put them in a basket. "Come, my son. Do you want to go help me check traps while your mother sews with Mar-lenn?"

"No," Analay says brightly. "There's nothing in the traps."

Zolaya pauses and looks at his mate, who purses her lips. After a moment, Zolaya speaks again. "If there is nothing in the traps, then we will gather herbs for your mother's tea."

"Okay." Analay gets up and heads to his bed, pulling his furs out of the basket of clothing. He begins to dress and Zolaya moves to his side while Ariana glances down at the baby at her breast.

I move inside, pulling out my folding stool from its spot in the corner next to my sewing basket. With her pregnancy (and now new *bébé*) making her slow, we sew at her hut so she does not have to walk the extra steps to mine. "Can I get you something? Food? Tea? Cookies?"

Analay brightens at the word "cookies" but wrinkles his nose when I show them the flavor. Even so, he is a kit and takes one, nibbling on it with a woeful expression. Ariana fights back a laugh, her eyes full of sympathy as Zolaya helps their son dress in enough layers for the blustery day. When they are ready, they both kiss Ariana goodbye, and I don't miss the way she reaches up and touches Zolaya's braid, a soft smile in her eyes.

Then they are gone and it is just me, Ariana and new baby Zoari, and a basket full of terrible herby-sweet cookies. I eat one absently even as I pull out my scattered bits of leather. I was working on a fitted tunic for Farli, but since she shows no signs of returning home anytime soon, I will put it aside and work on something new. "Borran gave me new leather," I tell Ariana. "I am going to make a sack-dress for Zoari."

"Okay?" She smiles, but there is a question in her eyes.

"*Oui.*" I dig through my sewing basket, and then sigh with frustration. "No cord. Why is there never cord when I need it? *Alors.*" For a moment, I purse my lips at the leather bits in my arms and then fling them all into the basket.

Ariana slips a finger between Zoari's little blue mouth and her skin, breaking the suction, and then lifts the baby to her shoulder, rubbing the small back. I can see that Zoari has the soft markings of the sa-khui protective plating along her small spine.

My Zalene has that, too, and for a moment I'm hit with fierce longing and a rush of worry.

"Are you all right?" Ariana's voice is gentle. "You don't seem to be yourself today."

I drum my fingers on my leg, feeling oddly restless. I have the leather I need. I'm sure Ariana has extra cord, and I keep needles in my belt pouch, but for some reason, I pick up the basket of scraps and begin to pull them out, smoothing them onto my lap and straightening them out. It takes me a minute before I realize what I'm doing—I'm looking for hearts. For a sign from my mother's spirit that all is still well and I'm just imagining things. But they're just shapes, and nothing calls out to me. I glance up and Ariana's still watching me, her brows knit in concern.

"*Je suis inquiète*," I tell her, and when she continues to look at me blankly, I realize I lapsed into French. "I worry."

She gives me an easy, teasing smile, rubbing Zoari's back in little circles. "You? You are Marlene. You never worry." Her amused boast makes me smile despite myself, and she continues. "Even on the day we were dropped onto this strange world, you never worried. We ran around screaming like banshees and crying for weeks, but you just smiled and acted like this was just another day."

I think of that day, of seeing my Zennek's face for the first time, and a dreamy smile touches my lips. "*C'était une bonne journée.*"

She snorts. "For you, maybe. My anxiety was through the roof for weeks." The baby belches and her little tail flicks contentedly. Ariana swaddles her and then slowly rocks her in her arms, coaxing her drowsy-eyed daughter to sleep. When she speaks again, her voice is softer, so as not to wake the baby. "I'm serious, though. What's troubling you? You can tell me. As your friend, I know something's on your mind. Is it Zalene?"

"Non. My little *cocotte* is her usual happy self." I think for a minute, smoothing a scrap of leather on my lap and then sigh. Now that I have to mention my worries to someone else, it seems silly. "I am seeing bad omens today."

"Bad omens?"

"*Oui.* Zalene stepped in animal dung with her right foot when we were out this morning, and then I thought I saw bread—but not bread, of course, there is no bread here—turned upside down." I shake my head. "It sounds crazy, I know."

"I'm not going to tell you that you're crazy. This is me here." Her smile is gentle. I know what she's thinking—of everyone in the tribe, Ariana struggles to fit in the most. She suffers from a great anxiety in her head, and sees the healer often because her khui cannot conquer bad thoughts. She always worries the other women in the tribe dislike her, which is not true. But if anyone will understand foolish worries, it is her.

"It sounds foolish when I say it aloud, but my *Maman*, she always paid attention to omens."

She studies the baby in her arms, and Zalene's little mouth works in her drowsy almost-sleep, as if she's still nursing. "You should have said and we could have asked Analay." Ariana thinks for a moment and then shakes her head. "Then again, maybe not. He makes things up because he's little, too. Like yesterday? He told me quite seriously that the dirtbeaks were going to school to learn how to give us better eggs. And the day before he told me it was going to snow so hard it'd be like a blanket." She gestures at the air. "No snow."

Mmm. She has a point. It is so cold that the air hurts to breathe, but there is no snow and has not been for several days. "The omens do not bother me as much as that I do not see anything from my *Maman*. Always she has sent me signs, but today I look and look and see nothing." I chew on my lip, worried.

"Does she normally send you signs every day?"

"Not every day, no."

"But you need them today and you're not seeing them," Ariana guesses correctly, and I nod. "I understand."

I pick another piece of leather out of the basket and add it to the growing pile in my lap. I need to keep my hands busy or I will wring them like a 50s movie heroine. "Do you think I worry overmuch?"

"It's possible?" She eases to her feet, carefully cradling the now sleeping baby as she moves toward the basket of furs next to her bed. When Zoari is settled and sleeping, she moves back toward me and sits down again, picking up a long-cold cup of tea and swallowing it all. She dips a fresh cup and then studies me, leaning back. "Do you think your brain could just be feeding you things to worry over? I mean, I stress every brutal season. The weather can really beat you down, and I know food stores are going to get low in about two months like they always do, but we go through this every brutal season, and I remind myself that we always come out the other side. Do you think that could be what it is?"

"*Je ne sais pas.*" I shrug. "Perhaps I am broody, or my period is about to start."

"Or...you're going to resonate?" Her eyes go wide. "A lot of people are having second resonances right now and maybe it's your turn."

I chuckle at that. "Come, now, we both know how I acted when I resonated to Zennek. I was not full of worry."

She gives me a mischievous smile, grinning. "No. I remember you watched him like a very hungry spider and he was the fattest fly ever just wandering close to your web."

I laugh, full of delight. Am I such a predator? Only when it comes to my shy, handsome Zennek. He brings out the fierce tigress in me. Pleased, I think of my handsome mate and how he looked that day, his long hair pulled back in a tight, stern braid...that I immediately loosened.

I think I shall loosen his braid for him tonight and perhaps we will be tigress and prey once more. A sultry smile curls my mouth and I look over at my friend. "I think perhaps I see worry where there is none." Already talking to her about this makes me feel better.

"If it helps, Analay would have said something when he saw you. He hasn't figured out how to tactfully point out things yet. He told Josie that he always saw her fat. I nearly had a heart attack, but Josie just laughed." She shakes her head, her expression exasperated. "But you know with his 'knowing' if he saw something bad, he would have spoken up."

Hmm, she has a good point. "*Bon.* I will put it aside then, like so much bad leather." I wink at her and toss a handful of scraps back into their basket. "Now, shall I make your pretty *cocotte* a sack-dress? This new leather is very soft." And I unroll it for her to see.

Hours later, Zoari wakes up for another feeding and Ari takes care of her while I continue to sew. When the baby finally goes down for another nap, Ariana starts to yawn, and I finish the stitches on the downy-soft sleeves of the simple sack-dress that I've sewn together. Ariana and I have passed the time talking and sewing, comparing stories of mates and kits as married friends do. My mind is no longer full of distress and instead, I find that I am getting sleepy, too.

"I think I might take a nap while Zoari does," Ariana tells me as she puts her sewing aside. "Zoari isn't as fussy as Analay was, but that still doesn't mean she's sleeping through the night."

"*Bien sûr.* I might take one myself." I fight back another yawn. The kits' "school" is temporarily on hold while Ariana has a new baby, and Gail is gone to Icehome, which means that I do not have many afternoons to myself. This one will be a treat and I can lie about and rest until my handsome Zennek and sweet Zalene return home. I gather up my sewing, straighten up the hearth with Ariana, and then kiss her cheeks as I leave. "*À plus.*"

It's a short walk back to my own hut and chilly inside, because I've let the fire go down to coals as I visited others. I stoke it, add a chip of the slow-burning dvisti dung, and then move to my bed, burrowing under the thick furs for warmth. I close my eyes, reveling in the quiet and peace of the afternoon.

A nice, lazy day, my mother would say. The chores can wait a few hours, and I will treat myself with a pleasant nap. So I close my eyes, snuggle in to my bed, and wait to drift off to sleep.

I don't, though. Instead, I wake up and stare up at my ceiling. I gaze up at the smoke hole that lets the thread of smoke out of my hut. I look up at the tented roof made of waterproofed skins that have been carefully pieced together. It is very different from the day I first arrived.

Very different.

And I cannot stop thinking about that day.

Or Zennek.

2

MARLENE

Eight Years Ago

I STARE up at the harsh metal ceiling overhead. It's unfamiliar and this place is so intensely cold that it feels as if my breath will freeze in my lungs. Not Fort Lauderdale, then. I am somewhere new, somewhere strange. Around me, women weep and sob, and someone wails about how cold they are. How frightened.

I suppose I would be frightened, too, but as I look up, I stare at the metal ceiling. There are scorch marks all over it, as if it went through a terrible trauma, and I cannot help but notice that one scorch mark looks like a heart.

Always with the hearts.

I see you, *Maman. Je me souviens.*

Even though I am in this forbidding, cold place, I am safe. She is reassuring me that I have nothing to fear, and I am calm as I sit up. We are supposed to be sleeping, us humans, because tomorrow we venture out into the snow and toward the home *des barbares*. I look at the group of women near me. Many weep. One trembles with fear. Several are sickly and weak, and I wince in sympathy at the sight of a fragile girl with a heavily splinted leg and a pinched look of pain on her face. Some of them are wounded and starving, and one girl has frostbite on her toes. I have no such problems. I was in a deep sleep, Georgie said to me. A stasis. Half the girls were in stasis and the other half were not so lucky. They froze and starved out here in the broken remains of the spaceship while Georgie tried to find help.

It seems she found help all right.

My gaze slides away from the other human women to the blue-skinned strangers. They watch us unabashedly, their expressions fascinated. You would almost think they had never seen a female before, *là*. Georgie gets up from our group and approaches the one that I think is their leader, and they share a kiss while he watches her possessively. It seems Georgie found more than just a friend. That's *un petit ami* if I have ever seen one. Perhaps I should find one for myself.

I make a game out of such a thought, studying the aliens as if I am choosing one for my own personal pleasure. After all, I cannot sleep with the sobbing and misery around me. There is no television or books, nothing to do or look at except the heart smeared into the ceiling that tells me that *Maman* watches over me even now.

So I roll onto my side, prop up on an elbow, and scrutinize the aliens.

They have blue skin, which is *incroyable*. Some are darker blue than others, and when Georgie pets her blue man's arm, I wonder if he is soft to the touch. Interesting. Many of them are shirtless, wearing nothing but loincloths that outline some VERY interesting anatomy. Ah, *Maman,* what a place to be stranded! If every male here is built as if he is a hulking bull, I will be a very happy Marlene indeed. One turns away to whisper to another, and I notice a flicking tail, much like a cat's. Fascinating. I want to touch one. I wonder if that would be considered rude. I shall have to ask.

I study the big, arching horns that they have. Some are curling and thick, some are sleek, and some curve close to the brow as if caressing the head. They all have big, oversized features and hard brows, and bright, glowing blue eyes. As I watch, the two whispering to each other glance over at me. How I must look to them, all pale white skin and black, rumpled hair. Skinny arms and short body. They are all immensely tall with thick, three-toed feet and broad shoulders.

I wink at the one that caught me staring. His nostrils flare and he looks displeased, glancing away. I chuckle inwardly. That one is not a friend then. Eh. He is too tall for my tastes, his mouth turned down in unpleasant lines. I continue studying the aliens and my gaze locks down on one carrying a stack of rolled-up furs toward the group of blubbering, terrified females. I watch him with interest, and when he glances over at me, I wink, testing this one as well.

He practically stumbles over his feet, staggering. When he straightens, I notice the bases of his horns have flushed a deep, velvety blue.

Oh now, this is interesting.

I sit up, clutching my blanket to my chest, and snap my fingers at him to get his attention. "*Coucou, mon ami!*"

The hulking giant glances around, then carefully looks over his shoulder as if expecting to see me talk to someone else. I cannot help but laugh. "I speak to you, my blue friend. *Viens ici.*" I make a gesture that he should come forward.

Again he looks around, and then gives the group what can only be described as a downright bashful look. He comes toward me and holds out one rolled-up fur in silence.

I pat the cold, metal floor next to me, indicating that he should sit and keep me company. And I smile, because what man would resist a naked female smiling at him? I am not going to fuck him, of course. I am just having a little bit of fun.

This one, apparently, can resist a naked female who smiles at him. He drops the blanket in front of me, manages another bashful look, and then hurries away. I chuckle, taking the blanket, and use it as a pillow under my cheek as I watch him leave. I like the way the shy one looks, I decide. He is not as tall as some of the others but *la*, he is wide, his arms great big blue slabs of muscle veined with power. His back is thick and broad and tapers down to narrow hips that have a small loincloth clinging to them. I watch that backside in fascination.

Oh yes. If I were picking myself an alien, I would pick that shy one. It would be fun to see how many ways I could make him blush. I am not normally such a...hungry woman when I am at home, but *là,* do the men at home look like these? Never. Every one of them ripples with muscle and confidence. They are tall and strong and utter perfection. I gaze at the shy one again, noting the incredibly tight weave of the braid that goes down his back. I wonder if his hair is soft, or if he ever loosens it.

He glances back over at me and then quickly looks away once more, and I cannot help but smile.

A sobbing girl thumps down next to me, huddled in blankets.

Her face is the picture of misery. I automatically sit up to make room for her, and put an arm around her shoulders. She leans in and weeps on my arm as I stroke her hair. "Why are you not freaking out?" she asks me. "Aren't you s-scared?"

Am I? I glance around the room, assessing the situation for what feels like the hundredth time today. The aliens—the barbarians —are huddled on the far side, whispering and talking. Two are guarding the entrance to our dirty, cold metal home and they hold crude-looking spears. Off to one side, Georgie—the American with the bouncy curls and authoritative expression—curls up next to her alien. I see the way he watches her as she relaxes against him. He looks at her like I look at a fresh baked croissant covered in butter. I watch as one big hand gently touches Georgie's hair, and the look on his face is reverent with joy.

I am not afraid of these aliens, no. We are here for a reason. What that reason is, I do not know, but I am not afraid. I pat my companion on the shoulder, noticing that amongst the muddy boot-prints that cover the floor, there is one that looks like an elongated heart shape. It reassures me that this is the right way to think. "There is no reason to panic, *mon amie*. We are in good hands."

She looks at me as if I am crazy. "But did you hear what they said? There's no going home! We're stuck here! And there's nothing but snow and ice on this planet."

Maman always did like the snow. And a new adventure. Did we not get on the Métro every weekend to visit new cities? Did we not travel all over Europe because *Maman* loved to explore? That was what I was doing when I ended up here—adventuring in the States. Perhaps that is why she is reassuring me all is well—it is just another adventure. I smile at the heart on the ground and shrug. "It is just a new adventure for us."

"I don't want adventure," she wails. "I want to go home!"

I sigh. I did not choose this adventure either, but that does not mean it will be a bad one. It is a big change, and if I think about it too hard, it will be frightening...so I will not think. "Let us sleep, hmm? It will all seem less scary *demain matin*—in the morning."

3

ZENNEK

𝓘 do not know what I expected when my chief told us we would be helping him retrieve "hoo-man" females. He returned from his hunts with a strange creature on his back, a female that he claimed was his mate, and no one could believe it. But he was resonating to her even though she had no khui yet, so it was clearly true. We set off to rescue the females, and even though I knew that was our task, the sight of so many was...over-whelming.

Even now, my tongue feels tied into a hard knot as I hand out rolled-up furs to the weeping creatures. They all seem to be upset and shivering, and nearby, Aehako makes hot tea in front of the fire and hands out warm cups of it to try and settle the hoo-mans. I can tell by the smell that he has added a calming herb, but it does not seem to be working yet.

Only two of the females are not panicked by their situation— Shorshie, Vektal's mate, and the one with hungry eyes who watches me. I kneel down and pretend to adjust the laces on my boot, and as I do, I steal a glance over at her. She still watches me, her strange, dark eyes avid. When our gazes meet, she purses her lips in my direction and then chuckles to herself. I do not know what that gesture is but...watching her strange pink lips makes my cock stir. Flustered, I jerk to my feet and move to the back of the cave, where my brothers lean against the wall and talk in low voices. Pashov and Salukh glance at me as I approach, my tail lashing.

"That one rattles you," Pashov tells me with a grin, nudging his chin at the hungry-eyed female. "Your brow is flushed like a young hunter with his cock newly erect."

I give him an irritated shove, but his words just make my face heat even more. I look over at Salukh, my capable, always-settled brother. He does not look flustered by the females. "Do...you think it is resonance?"

Salukh snorts. "How should I know?" His mouth curves into a wry smile. "My chest is as silent as it ever was."

I glance at Pashov. He rubs his chest, expression thoughtful and distracted. He does not look at my female, though, but at another. Of course, the realization that I think of her as "my female" makes me restless and uncomfortable all over again.

To think that I might have a female when all of this is settled. To think that we all might. It is...incredible. "You are calm, Salukh," I point out. "My heart races at the sight of the females. Pashov looks similarly affected, but you do not. Tell me your secret." I want to know how to remain calm so the smiles of the one with the dark mane and enticing eyes do not make my tongue attach itself to the roof of my mouth.

My unruffled brother shrugs. "Resonance decides," Salukh says.

"If I am to have a female, I will resonate. Until that happens, they are just new tribesmates, nothing more."

New tribesmates. Of course. But that is not such a simple thought either. We are a small tribe. New tribesmates are born, and ever since the khui sickness, the births are few and far between.

It is not as easy as all that. "Mm." I look to Pashov to see what he thinks, but he is lost in thought yet, his gaze fixed on the females. I turn and try to see who he stares at, but as night approaches and the temperature drops, the females huddle together for warmth near the fire, piled together like snowcat kits. It is impossible to tell who has captured his attention, but I will ask later.

A male approaches us—my chief. Even he is different now that he has resonated to the small, pale hoo-man called Shorshie. There is a sparkle in his eye, a spring to his step. There is hope that lightens the weight on his shoulders. He approaches me and my brothers and leans in, speaking in a low voice. "The hoo-mans cannot stay here. We must find a sa-kohtsk and hunt them khuis, and then we must take them to the elders' cave so they can receive our words like Georgie did." He pauses to look at his mate with a possessive expression. "We leave in the morning at first light."

I nod. Morning, because the travel will be slow with so many sickly and weak females. They are not like my sister, Farli, who is strong and tall despite her young age. These seem far more fragile, more likely to break at a strong wind. How does it not terrify my chief to be mated to such a delicate creature?

"Would sleds not be better?" Salukh asks, ever practical. He crosses his arms over his chest and studies Vektal. "We could take another day or two, get some bones from one of the hunter caves and make several of them so the hoo-mans can ride."

The chief shakes his head. "Some of the hoo-mans are very sick.

The air is poisoning them because they have no khui. We must go and go soon. First light."

It makes sense. "Of course, my chief."

He studies me, and then Pashov. "Because the hoo-mans are so weak, I am asking all the hunters to find one and watch over her. Take her under your wing and make sure she stays warm. Make sure she can keep up and that she wears enough furs...and make sure that she stays with the rest of the group. I cannot watch all of them. Carry a female if you must, but we need them all together for when we find the sa-kohtsk."

"Understood," Pashov says, his expression focused once more. "We will not fail you."

Vektal nods at my brothers and then heads off to talk to Haeden, who is already scowling with displeasure. He will not like being told to watch over a hoo-man, I think. Then again, he does not like much of anything.

Pashov flings an arm around my shoulders. I am shorter than him, and he does this to point out this fact. I try to shrug him off, but he only grabs me in a headlock and grins. "Which one are you going to pick, little brother?"

I growl at him. Pashov is tall, and Salukh is massive and broad. I am neither, but that does not mean I am puny. The words "little brother" make me irritated, especially in front of the females. "Do not make me break your nose again."

Salukh barks a laugh, and Pashov immediately releases me. "You said that was an accident!"

"It was. This time it will be on purpose." I give him a light shove. "As for the females, I do not know."

It is a lie. I do know—I want the one with hungry eyes—but I do not know if I am brave enough to approach her.

Pashov looks over at Salukh.

He shrugs. "It matters not to me."

"I want the one with the big teats," Pashov says, his expression suddenly fierce. "The big teats and brown mane. Stay away from that one."

Big teats and brown mane? I look at the cluster of females and see one that I suspect matches that description, but she does not look particularly enticing to me. Pashov watches her with an intensity that makes me wonder, though. "She is yours," I tell him.

"You should claim the one with hungry eyes," Pashov tells me, breaking his gaze long enough to look over at me.

I can feel my face grow hot again. My tail thrashes and I just shrug, imagining her pink mouth in a curving smile as she looks at me...and then I am too awkward to speak.

"Someone else will claim her if you do not," Pashov warns me.

The thought is absurd. There are so many females that it makes my head spin...and yet the thought of her giving her enticing smiles to Dagesh or Haeden or Aehako makes my head spin. Fierce possessiveness ripples through me and I cross my arms over my chest, frowning as I look over at the females once more, seeking out the black mane of the female in question.

The moment I see her, I realize she is still watching me. I look away again.

"She watches you," Salukh tells me, amused.

Even though I do not want to, I turn to look over at her again. She wiggles her strange eyebrows in my direction and traces a shape on the floor, her fingertip moving over the flat metal cave in an enticing manner that makes my cock respond. I look away again.

"You should talk to her," Salukh encourages. "Perhaps she is interested in a pleasure mating."

My brother makes it sound as if it is the easiest thing in the world to discuss. Pleasure mating. It is something that I have always wanted yet never thought would happen for me. A pleasure mating. A hand on my cock other than my own? I think of the female. She would not weep and whimper at the thought of mating. She would welcome me with hot eyes and a smile. I bite back the strangled sound that rises in my throat and hope my loincloth hides my erection. "I will talk to her...soon."

"When? She still watches you."

"Soon," I say again quickly, and then stalk away from my brothers so they do not pester me with more questions. I head to the front to relieve one of the hunters guarding the entrance, just because it will give me an excuse to avoid the females and my brothers both.

I am not on guard for long before Aehako comes out and gives me a nudge. "Go inside. We are all taking quick turns so we have an opportunity to watch the hoo-mans."

I want to protest that the hoo-mans are why I am out here, but...I do want to look at them more. At one in particular. I avert my gaze and pull my hood over my horns so he does not see the blush staining my brow. I return inside, and I am disappointed that the female with the hot eyes and dark mane is asleep, curled under the blankets against all the others. But since she is sleeping...this gives me a chance to look at her without embarrassment. I approach, pretending to add another chip of fuel to the fire, then stoke it with the bone left next to the stones for such a purpose. As I do, I look at her, drinking in her features. Up close, her face is small, her features tiny compared to my own. Her nose is but a snub, the brows she wiggles at me small slashes of dark above her expressive, odd eyes. It is her mouth that fascinates me the most, how pink and wet it seems. Her lips are full and pleasant, and her pale skin is an ugly color but it looks...soft. Her eyes flutter and then she is looking at me.

I should greet her. Be kind. Reassure her that all is well. Speak hoo-man to her.

Instead, all that comes out is a strangled sound, like the honking of a scythe-beak in mating flight.

She makes a soft sound of amusement and then pats the open floor next to her, as if inviting me to sit. I blink, and then hastily move away again. *Coward,* I tell myself. *Coward! She is but a small female. Why do you run?*

But I know why I run. I know my tongue will remain tangled, and my cock will throb and I will not be able to speak. I will end up scaring her more than reassuring her. I move to the far end of the strange stone cave and clench my fists, trying to calm my thoughts. *Go back to her,* I tell myself. *Go back and greet her. Say "ho." It is the easiest sound to make. She will not bite. She will not laugh at you—she likes you, does she not?*

One of the humans makes a startled cry, and then everyone is on alert. "They're coming back," one of the humans says. "We have to go, now!"

4

ZENNEK

*T*here is a mad scramble as we rush to get the humans away from the cave. Other aliens will be coming back to snatch them away from us, tracking them from devices embedded in their arms that flash under the skin. I have never seen anything like it, but when Shorshie digs hers out of her arm and reveals it to be a bit of metal, I realize what they are saying is true. Soon, all the humans go under the knife, some crying, most grim-faced and silent as they are wounded and bandaged. As the humans have the strange flashing rock removed from their arms, they are immediately bundled up by those of us waiting nearby. I have a bundle of boots that were retrieved from our stores and hand a pair to each female as she passes by.

One small female has a bad leg and her tone is hysterical. "Please don't leave me behind!" She casts us worried looks, her eyes full of tears.

Haeden gives her a look of disgust. He snatches the boots from my grip and scoops the small female into his arms. "I will carry this one."

She flings her arms around his neck, sobbing her relief, and Haeden just looks even more displeased.

A familiar thrumming sound touches my ears. The throb of it is faint...but I know it. I look around, and as I do, Pashov's gaze meets mine. He puts a hand over his chest, a look of wonder on his face.

My brother resonates. I am filled with joy for him. At his side, Dagesh touches his chest, watching one of the human females swaddled in furs by the entrance.

"Who is it?" I ask my brother, moving close.

"The female I liked. I knew it." He casts a grin in my direction. "Say nothing, though. I do not want her to be scared. She needs time."

And we need to retreat from this place. I nod at him and steal a glance over at Dagesh. Does he resonate to *my* female?

But no, she stands, waiting for her arm to have the strange pellet removed. A wave of relief rushes through me.

Vektal stalks through our group like a protective father. He puts a hand on my chest, pauses, and then moves on to Pashov. My brother immediately bats Vektal's hand away, and my chief scowls at him. He leans in. "Let the hoo-mans make the first move."

Pashov nods.

The last of the humans have the strange flickering thing removed from their arm, and then they are bundled up. Vektal takes the pouch of the location-pebbles and hands it to Pashov. "Take this away from here and drop it into the nearest metlak cave."

Pashov looks at the females, then back at his chief and nods. I know he wants to stay. It is in the stubborn set of his shoulders, but he does as Vektal commands. I suspect Vektal deliberately sent my brother away because he resonates.

Then we are out in the snow. Vektal hefts his mate onto his back and takes the lead, gesturing for the rest of us to follow. One by one, we pair up with the females, some males taking on the responsibility of watching over two as they currently outnumber us. Haeden carries his broken-legged female on his back, and I heft my backpack then look at the females, trying to find one in particular.

A hand taps my arm. "*Salut.*"

I turn, and it is the female with the hot eyes. They are not so hot right now, though, but full of fear. She shivers as she looks at me, waiting patiently. I automatically pull my light cloak off of my shoulders and wrap it around her. The snow drifts down, but otherwise it is a pleasant day, yet she shivers and trembles as if it is deep in the brutal season. "Ho," I manage to choke out.

"May I walk with you?" she asks, and she says hoo-man words strangely, as if her tongue is caressing them. Fascinated, I watch her mouth for a moment, then nod, blushing. "*Merci.*" She puts a hand on my arm and steps forward, only to sink into the deep snow.

"I...can...carry you," I manage to choke out in hoo-man tongue. It is hard to look directly at her when she watches me. She is so... fragile and lovely. The strange color of her skin and her small features grow more appealing by the moment, and I can feel my brow is on fire with my blush.

She pauses. "If you are sure? I can walk." And she tries to step forward again, this time losing her boot in the snow. "*Merde,*" she says, and the sound is annoyed. It is another hoo-man word, and one I do not recognize. I rub my ear, wondering if perhaps the hoo-man words did not go into my brain properly as they did the others.

I will worry about that later, though. I bend to retrieve her boot and hold it out so she can put her small foot inside it. She does, and I automatically lace it up her calf, making sure it is tight so it will not slide off again.

Her hand goes to my back and I stiffen.

"*Oh, mon Dieu,*" she murmurs, her fingers stroking over my shoulder. "*Tu es si doux.*"

My cock reacts, hardening immediately, and the breath whooshes from my lungs. I make a "guh" sound and then clear my throat. "We must walk."

"Apologies," she says, but she does not sound sorry. She sounds amused. "Perhaps it is best if you carry me after all." She looks ahead at the others, who are already outpacing us.

I nod and remain bent in the snow, patting my shoulder so she can climb onto me like Farli used to do as a kit. Her arms go around my neck and the scent of her fills my nose. There is a strange scent to her skin that reminds me of the liquid that covered her in the pods, but under that, she smells musky and pleasant and my cock feels like stone even as it thrusts against the leather of my loincloth. I am glad she is on my back, because now she cannot see that, at least.

I draw in a breath to brace myself and then get to my feet. Her legs curl around my waist and her arms are chokingly tight, but I do not complain. I like the feel of her against me, and I jog forward to catch up with the others, hoping that my erection will die down before anyone else notices.

Then again, this is the first time we have all been around so many unmated females. I am probably not the only one with an aching cock.

We walk for a time, and I say nothing. Some of the others chat with their humans as they encourage them to walk faster— Aehako is talking the ear off of two of the females, and Rokan is in conversation with another while Zolaya grins and tells a silly story, doing his best to make a weeping one stop her crying.

"*Je suis Marlène*," the female says in my ear. Her breath tickles against my skin and I shudder, immediately shocked at how much that brush of her breath affects me. "*Et toi?*" she prompts, and pats my shoulder with one thickly-gloved hand.

She seems to want something, but I do not know what she asks. "Can you speak hoo-man?" I ask her. It is easier to talk to her when I stare ahead and try not to think of how close she leans in, or her pink mouth so near to my ear...

And now I am hard again. I furtively rub a hand against my cock, willing it to subside.

The female chuckles into my ear. "There is more than one human language, silly man. Perhaps it is you that is not speaking the words correctly."

That draws me up short. I pause, worried. "I am not?"

"Keep walking," she tells me with a tap to my shoulder. "I do not want to be left behind."

Of course. I pick up my feet again and continue. I must get her away from the strange cave. We do not have time for me to pause and get flustered by her words.

"I tease you," she tells me in that soft, lilting voice. "I am sorry if it was confusing. My tongue is different than the others'."

"Different?" I ask, because I must. I caught a glimpse of it earlier—pink and wet—but I did not notice it being different than the other humans. "Is that why you sound different from them?"

"*Oui.* Ahem, yes."

Well, that explains a great many things. She is still interesting, for all that her mouth has a strange tongue in it. "Say no more. I will tell the others not to mock you."

"Mock...me?"

"Because of your odd tongue."

She chuckles into my ear again. "Oh, I like you, *mon ami.* You are adorable."

I know that word, and I can feel the base of my horns flushing with heat. I deliberately slow my steps so we can be at the back of the group, so no others will see my erection and wonder what things she says to me with her unusual tongue.

"I tried to give you my name," she continues when I do not speak up. "It is Marlene."

"Mar-lennnn," I echo, trying to pronounce it like she does. "I am called Zennek."

"It is a pleasure to meet you, Zennek," she whispers against my neck, her breath tickling my skin, and it sends a shiver right to my groin. Even the way she says my name is...enticing.

She makes me wonder, this Mar-lenn. I grow bold enough to ask her a question. "May I ask you something?"

"Of course."

"You do not scream and cry like the others. Are you not afraid?"

She is silent for a moment, as if contemplating my words. "Would you prefer that I squeal and cling to you in terror so you can feel brave?"

I think for a moment. "No. I would rather you not be afraid. We mean you no harm." I want to tell her that I like her smiles, but that feels too bold, and I am not yet that bold around such a strange female.

"I am worried, *oui,* because I would be a fool to not have worry. This is a new place and it is very cold and strange. But I am not scared, *non.* Look." She points at the ground.

I see nothing but footprints, and wait for her to indicate what I am supposed to be seeing.

"Those two boot prints have come together at the heel. Like a heart." She says it softly, full of wonder. "That tells me I am safe here."

She thinks boot prints will keep her safe? I worry that her brain is just as strange as her tongue, but I say nothing. I do not wish to hurt her feelings.

Perhaps I have already said too much.

5

MARLENE

$\mathcal{Z}$ ennek is skittish around me.

He is a gentleman, of course. All of the *grands hommes bleus* are. They are careful with us right down to the last crying female, and when they hunt down the large creature they call a sa-kohtsk, they make sure we are safely hidden out of the way so no harm can come to us. Then, we are given the khui—the parasite. I do not remember much of that, just of one of the men holding a knife to my neck and nicking me. Something cool slithered against my throat.

Then...sleep.

When I woke up, there was a campfire. I moved toward it and counted heads. Two of the women seem to be missing, which is strange. I realize that one is Georgie...and perhaps it is not so strange after all. I do not know who the other missing one is. I touch my neck as I slowly wake up, but I do not hurt. In fact, I feel...nice. Comfortable. The air no longer shocks me with the bitterness of it. It will never be pleasant, but now the discomfort is mild and my furs make up for it. I move closer to the fire and sit next to the other women, watching as they chatter and talk to one another, sharing introductions. I am the only Frenchwoman, and I feel very different from the others. I continue to rub my neck thoughtfully as I look around, searching blue faces for a familiar one with a tight braid and a bashful expression.

Sure enough, there is Zennek, watching me from the far side of the encampment. He immediately ducks his head at the sight of me.

I cannot help but smile. *Là*, but he is shy. Georgie said they did not have many females, which seemed to be odd to me. But now that I have met Zennek? I believe it. I have never met one so very shy and yet so very masculine. He bulges with muscle but will not look me in the eye as if it is too difficult for him.

It's...surprisingly endearing. Sweet. There is something pure about his reactions to me...and my reaction to him is very much not pure.

I want to filthy him up.

I want to see if he will blush even with kisses.

I want to see if he blushes if I touch his cock, or take him into my mouth. I want to see his reaction when he touches me. Or when I touch him. Or when we try a variety of sexual positions...

My thoughts are positively scorching. I fan my face, my thoughts making my body heat.

"Are you too warm?" someone asks beside me. Nora, I think.

I shake my head. "Just...thinking about stuff."

"I understand." She rubs her chest, her own expression one of distraction as she gazes into the fire. "I'm having a hard time concentrating on much of anything."

I feel that as well. There is something inside me that feels as if it is unfurling, waking up for the first time, and I wonder if we are all supposed to feel this. If it is natural with this *nouvel ami*, the khui. I don't know and I'm not sure who to ask. Perhaps Zennek.

Or perhaps I am just looking for excuses to talk to him.

I keep thinking about how soft his skin was, how warm his big, strong body was under mine as he carried me. He hefted me on his back for hours, never tiring, never complaining. It was as if I weighed nothing to him, and the thought is an arousing one. I am drawn to strength, and he has it by the fistful.

I glance over at him again and as I do, heat throbs through my body. My nipples prick and I shift on my seat. I'm sitting on a rock near the fire, which means my backside is cold, but parts of me feel...liquid. Aching. Needy.

This is new.

I slide a hand between my thighs as if that will help the ache rising there.

"Where is Georgie?" someone asks, yawning.

I find it strange they can yawn. Should I be sleepy? I am not. Everything in me is utterly awake, and I steal another glance over at Zennek. He watches me from afar and this time, he doesn't duck his head or break eye contact. His blue glowing eyes lock with mine and it sends a ripple of...something through me.

"She has gone off to mate with Vektal," one of the tall blue ones tells her. "It is resonance."

Ah yes, the hunger for another that does not end until a mate has been claimed.

"What does resonance feel like?" Nora asks, and she is breathless beside me. Her gaze fixes on the male standing near the fire, and I notice his gaze is locked on her. "Does it make you tingle...everywhere?"

The male groans.

Nora jumps to her feet. Then, I hear it. We all hear it—like a drumbeat, Nora's chest is purring a loud rhythm that is matched by the alien across from her. He puts a hand out to Nora and she takes it, then flings herself into his arms.

With a groan, he grabs her ass, hauls her up against him, and then stalks out of the camp with her pressed to his front.

"Uh, should someone stop them?" asks a red-haired woman.

"It is resonance," one of the males remaining by the campfire says. "There is no stopping it." I notice envy in their looks as they watch Nora and her male storm away.

"I think I'm resonating, too," another woman says, getting to her feet. She is curvy, with a sweet face, and her eyes are wide as she stares at one of the males hovering nearby. For a moment, I think she will snatch up my Zennek, but I am relieved when a tall male approaches the fire and scoops her up into his arms, storming away.

So dramatic.

J'adore.

"Wow, this is crazy," someone says under their breath. "What's going on?"

"Resonance," several people tell her, and more than one sounds annoyed at having to repeat themselves.

The seats near me by the fire are empty, but no one is rushing to fill them. I wonder if Zennek will come sit with me if I wink and pat the stone next to me? Probably not. He is too shy.

I wonder why I am so obsessed with him. I rub between my thighs idly, then realize what I am doing. I am hot between my legs. No, more than that. I am practically dripping with need. Oh. I look across the fire at Zennek once more, and I know why I am so fascinated with him.

He is *mine*.

6

MARLENE

The rumble in my chest starts, deafening. It makes sense now, I think, and I cannot stop smiling as I get to my feet. Resonance. I know who it is, too. It is the shy, handsome one with the thick biceps and sturdy body that makes my mouth water. There are people whispering as I stand up, but I cannot hear their words. I do not care what they think. All I know is that Zennek should be touching me right now, and it is a shame that he is not.

I stride across the camp, holding my fur wraps against me as I approach him. He stands in place, frozen, his bright blue eyes locked on mine. There is no shyness in them now, only a startled expression as if he truly does not believe what he sees.

I reach forward, noticing that he has put on a thick tunic that hides his chest. Oh, I do not like this. I grab the front of the offending thing and then pull him down against me, pressing my mouth to his.

He does not kiss me back. He remains stiff and startled, and that is all right. I can show him how to kiss me. I can show him so many things. "Take me away from here, *mon beau*."

His expression dazed, Zennek gently takes me into his arms, then pulls his tunic off his head and drags it over mine. More clothing is...not what I wanted. Before I can sputter a retort, he hauls me into his arms and then strides out of camp with me over his shoulder.

Ah. That is much better.

I smile to myself even as I grab at his tight, fussy braid. Is all of him this tightly wound? I look forward to seeing him unleashed. I look forward to a great many things, actually. I press my cold fingers to my lips, thinking as I bob on his shoulder. He's silent, but he moves through the snowy night as if he knows where he is going, so I say nothing. I do not think I can talk over the insistent throb of my khui in my chest. It hammers a beat inside my body, and my pulse feels as if it moves in time with it. Heat fills my thighs, and my nipples rub against the leathers, making me crazy with need. I want to talk to Zennek when we arrive at...wherever we are going. I need to know more about resonance, what it means for us, but...it is terribly hard to think with the hunger rushing through my body. Georgie warned us. She said that the aliens told her resonance would mean a great, hungry need for another person that would not cease until mating was finished. I did not pay much attention, and now I wish I had, because the need for Zennek is consuming me. I want him to fling me down into the snow and ravish me. I want him to stop where we are, rip my leather pants off and bury his cock in my aching, liquid heat.

I want to ride him like a rollercoaster. I want to put my mouth all over his beautiful blue body and discover him with my tongue.

I want so, so many things, and I bite back a moan of hunger.

Zennek does not seem to be stopping anytime soon, but I can hear his khui singing in his chest, and his breath rasps in the night air. Before, he did not have trouble carrying me, but now he breathes heavy? Is he as affected as I am? Selfishly, I hope so. I squirm atop his shoulder, wishing he would slide a hand between my thighs and help me out as he walked.

Just thinking that practically makes me come.

"Where...are we going?" I manage, panting as well.

"Cave," he says, voice thick. "Hunter...cave."

"Close?" I ask.

He makes a sound that might be agreement. I hope it is close. I have never needed a man as badly as I need this one. I think about the kiss again. He did not kiss me back. Do his people not kiss? Or is it me he does not wish to kiss?

A new thought occurs to me.

If they do not have many females...this will all be new to him. He is the biggest, brawniest, sexiest virgin.

And he is mine.

I practically purr with the realization and drag my nails lightly along his rippling, muscled back. He jerks in response, and I can feel him go stiff under my shoulder. Then, he is panting hard once more even though he has stopped moving.

"Are we alone?" I ask. "Can we stop here, *mon beau*?" Because I do not want to wait until we are alone in a cave. I want him now. *Maintenant*.

"Soon," he manages, and I bite back words that my mother would have disapproved of. Instead, I run my hand down his naked back once more, pleased that all of this soft, velvety skin is right under my hands for the touching...and there it is.

Hard, bony plates trail up his back, and one directly over his tail-bone is in the shape of a heart. Of course it is.

Zennek is *mine*.

I practically purr with the pleasure this thought brings me, and I trace a finger over it. He asked before if I was afraid. I was not, because I knew *Maman* was watching over me. This heart? I do not care if it is something all his people have—I see it right now, and I know he is mine and we are meant to be. It is almost as if *Maman* has approved of him.

The thought fills me with joy. It feels good.

Almost as good as the needy heat rushing through my body. It pulses through me in time with my heartbeat and seems to grow stronger with every breath I take. The most frustrating thing is that Zennek does not seem to be stopping anytime soon. He keeps walking through the snow as if we must get somewhere important.

I let this go on for a time, but I grow impatient. I need...something. Relief, *certainement*. A break? That too. A snack? Answers to where we are going? Yes to all. So I pat my big alien on the back to get his attention. "Where do we go, *mon beau*?"

"Hunter cave," he tells me, as if that explains all.

"Is it far?"

"No."

Well, that is something at least. I look around, lifting my head, but I can no longer see the campfire in the distance where the others are huddled. We have gone far, I think, farther than I realized. How long have we been walking?

No one has stopped Zennek as he stole me away so they must be okay with this. The thought amuses me for some reason. They saved me from the bad aliens only to let this shy, beefy one steal me away so he can ravish me.

I am ready for my ravishment, though. Very ready.

I squirm on his shoulder, shifting my bottom and hoping he'll put a hand on it. "Are we there yet?"

"Not yet. Close."

Mais alors, this man misses all of my signals. I grab his braid and bring it to my face, brushing the tail of it against my cheek as I ride slung over his shoulder. His hair is thick and not soft like his skin—it feels more like cords than silk, but I like the texture of it all the same. I rub it against my lips and then breathe in its almost fruity scent. His hair smells like berries, which is odd, but I like it. I soon grow tired of toying with his hair and think as I run the tail of his braid over my face. I want his attention and I am not afraid to be bratty to get it. Cold hands down his tiny loincloth, perhaps? I let go of his braid and use my teeth to pull my gloves off my hands. Sneakily, I reach down just as his tail flicks back and forth, like a cat's. Oooh, interesting. I wonder if he will notice if I touch his tail.

Curious, I gently run a finger along the base of it.

Zennek makes a strange gargling sound and the world tips over. Astonished, it takes me a moment to realize what is happening, but then I hit the snow and flop onto my back. Did he...drop me?

I sit up, spitting snow and swiping it off of my face. I look over at him and *mon beau* lies entirely on his back, flat, his hands cupped in front of his loincloth. His brow is flushed—something I can see even in the dark—and he is breathing hard, his khui humming furiously.

And even though his hands are big, I can see that Zennek cannot entirely hide his...gifts under them.

Là. Now that is interesting.

"Did you trip?" I ask, amused. I lean closer to him and walk my fingers up one veiny bicep.

Skittish, he immediately rolls away and gets to his feet, not quite willing to face me. "Do not...no...tail..." he manages. "Not yet."

Ah. Tails are far more sensitive than I imagined, then. Feeling naughty, I smile into the darkness. "I will save it for later, then. Have we arrived?"

"Just over the next ridge," he tells me, gaze averted.

I get to my feet and dust off my furs. "*Bon*, let us go then."

No sooner do I stoop to scoop up my gloves than I am back in his arms again, this time carried like a bride toward the threshold. I fling my arms around his neck, but he won't look at me. His expression is...constipated. I want to giggle at how stoic he is trying to be. The more awkward and charming he is, the more playful it makes me.

"Is this a nice cave?" I ask him, sliding my hand down to his bare chest. Oh, I like being held in front of him much better than slung over his shoulder. Now I can caress him however I want... and I will have warning if he accidentally flings me into the snow again.

His mouth purses, practically in a frown. "Nice?"

"*Oui.* Is that why we go to it instead of making love in the snow right here? Because it is nice and romantic?" I roll the "r" in romantic dramatically even as I reach up to caress his jaw. Part of this is me being flirty and playful and having fun, and part of this is just blatant need for this big, sexy alien thanks to the khui humming insistently in my chest. I just want to touch him all over.

No, I amend silently. I *need* to touch him all over. It is worse than a craving, it is need. I feel as if I must, or this intense ache throbbing through me will never go away.

Zennek spares a look in my direction. "It is...a cave?"

Well, I knew that much. "I can mate in the snow if you promise to keep my derriere warm," I tell him, tracing my finger along his collarbone. My, but he's brawny.

He makes another strangled sound and then stares straight ahead, his footsteps seemingly quicker than before. "The cave...it has furs. Fuel. Food."

"The three Fs," I say, pretending to be solemn. "Very important. But you forgot F number four."

"Number four?"

"Fucking." I trace a finger around his nipple. Ooh, it's hard as a rock. "Though I suppose we will be bringing the fucking."

7

MARLENE

*H*is arms jerk around me and his breath sucks in even as his khui sings louder. For a moment, I think he's going to drop me—all because of a not-so-innocent nipple touch —but he recovers and keeps walking forward with grim determination. I smile to myself, because he is adorable in his virginal shyness.

For a long moment, there is nothing but the sounds of our khuis humming together in the darkness, and the whistle of the wind as it ruffles my hair. A few seconds later, though, I hear a new sound.

Groaning.

A woman's cries of need.

Someone is having sex up ahead.

Zennek realizes this at the same time I do and he halts in the snow, staring ahead with a frown.

"Is our cave occupied?" I ask, biting back my chuckle. He just looks so...stressed out. "Or shall we offer to join them?"

That gets a response out of him. He makes a hissing sound between his teeth and clenches me against his chest, tighter. "No. We do not join them. Not now. Not ever."

Aw. *Charmant.* I like this one more and more. "No, of course not," I soothe with a tiny pat on his possessive, possessive chest. "When you and I join together, it will be just us, *non*? Nice and private."

His gaze slides down to where my hand rests on the hard plating over his heart. Then, he looks over at me. There is an expression of yearning, of hard, hungry need in those eyes that takes my breath away.

Suddenly, I am less playful and more needy than ever before.

"Oh god. Just like that!" cries the woman from the cave, interrupting our tender moment. "Just like that, Dash!"

"It is Da-yesh," the man says, correcting her pronunciation.

"Daysh," she says again, full of need. "Put your mouth on me—"

"Close enough," the man says, but his words cut off and then the female cries out once more. It seems she is in no mood to be corrected and I bite back a giggle of amusement.

Zennek does not laugh. His breath comes quick through his nostrils, as if hearing the sounds of their lovemaking strains at his control. His hands tighten on me.

I tap a finger against his chest. "Is there another cave nearby?"

He blinks, then tears his gaze away from the distant cave and focuses on me. "No," he says, thickly. "There is one in another direction, but it will be occupied, too."

Ah. Two couples left before we did, and Georgie and her man as well. "I do not mind the snow," I tell him, trailing my finger up his chest.

"Privacy," is all he says, and then storms off in a new direction, and I bite back a sigh and hold onto his neck.

Luckily for me, he does not take me far. We half-skid down a slope into a rocky crevasse where the wind is less biting. Around us there are tumbled rocks, and in the distance, I hear water of some kind and then I pick up the faint smell of rotten eggs. A hot stream, then. I wrinkle my nose at the smell but do not complain, because at least now we no longer hear Dash or Dayesh or whatever his name is with his *petit-amour*. I can practically feel the tension in Zennek, though it has lessened now that we are farther away from them.

He sets me down gently into the snow and looks me over to make sure I am well. Then, he immediately gets to work, pushing and shoving at the snow near the base of one of the cliffs. It takes me a moment to realize what he is doing—he is making a wall of snow across from the cliff wall so we will be neatly enclosed and given a semblance of privacy. Clever.

"May I help?" I ask, getting to my knees as he digs handful after handful of snow in one direction, hollowing out a spot for our half-igloo.

"No," he says bluntly.

I rock back on my knees. Well, then. I sit back in the snow, watching him, and as he continues to work and the minutes stretch on, I yawn and lie on my side, propping my head up on one hand. Is he going to create an entire home out of snow and ice? Just to avoid being with me? There is no wind down here in the canyon, and with my furs—and his body heat pressed against mine—I will be warm enough, thanks to my khui. I watch him work feverishly and suspect that this industriousness is another aspect of his shyness. If he has a task, something to do with his hands, he does not have to look at me, non?

That wicked streak rises within me and I think of something naughty, something that will get his attention. Do I dare? Will he be angry? I watch him work feverishly for a moment longer, and then decide I will need to do something or else he will waste all of the night digging a pit into the snow as if it will somehow make his khui go silent.

So I clutch my belly and groan low, closing my eyes and doing my best to look as if I am in pain.

There's a mad scramble in the snow and then an impossibly warm hand touches my cheek. "Mar-lenn? Hoo-man? Are you well?"

I feel bad for what I am about to do, but only for a moment. "I hurt, Zennek. I hurt so badly." And I clutch at myself under my furs, curling my legs up as if protecting myself.

"How can I help?" His tone is worried but tender. He brushes my long hair off of my face and then touches one of my wrists, gently prying my hand away from my belly. "Show me where it hurts."

Reluctantly, I unfold my body and let him pull up my tunic. I shiver as he exposes my stomach to the air. "Hurts," is all I say, and I open my eyes to watch him.

He plasters one big blue hand against my bare skin and I moan at his touch, because it feels so very good. My sounds only worry him, though, because he gently kneads my belly. "Here?"

"Lower," I murmur.

8

MARLENE

*Z*ennek grabs at my leggings and rips the laces free, hauling them down my thighs. There's a worried expression on his face and it would almost be funny if I wasn't so damned...aroused.

He pauses at the sight of my mound and the dark curls there, and I can see his breathing quicken again. Can he see how wet I am?

"Where?" he asks, a gravelly tone in his voice, as if he is trying very hard to be good and pay attention even as my pussy is exposed before him.

"Inside," I tell him.

"Inside?"

"Yes." He leans closer as if to examine me, his breath practically on my skin, and I put a hand atop his head. "Now kiss it."

He jerks away from me so quickly that I can feel the wind rush past as he hauls himself backward. The look he shoots me is downright betrayed.

"You said you hurt," he accuses me.

"Oh, I do. I ache so badly." And I cup my pussy and give a little groan. "Do you not ache, *mon beau*?"

He scowls at me. His scowl deepens when I laugh. "This is not funny, hoo-man."

"Is it not? We should always be able to laugh at ourselves, *mon beau.*" I roll onto my back, gazing up at the stars. They're particularly brilliant here. I thought the clouds would obscure all of them, but there's no snow falling and the skies are littered with millions of stars and streaks of color. "You have to think this is a ridiculous situation, *non*?"

"How is it ridiculous?" I hear his voice from a short distance away, as if he's afraid to get too close to me.

I put a hand behind my head, not hitching up my pants. I keep my other hand on my pussy, because, well, it feels good. "I am a human. You are a blue alien. We are here on a planet that is nothing but snow, and very soon we will be having magnificent sex because a bug in my chest says it is so. And then I will have your *bébés.*"

"All of this is true."

I smile up at the stars, because just now I have noticed that one particular constellation looks like the shape of a heart. *You are everywhere, Maman.* "So. New planet. Bug. A mate. Babies. All because the bug says so. You do not think that is an odd situation?"

"Not to me."

Now he sounds hurt. I roll onto my side and regard him. Just as I suspected, he crouches a short distance away, tail flicking warily. "I said it was odd. I did not say it was bad, *mon beau*." I smile at him. "I like you. I am glad my khui chose you for me."

He frowns in my direction and says nothing for a long moment. When he speaks, he says, "Why me?"

"Why do I like you?" When he nods, I shrug and trace a heart into the snow before me. "You are strong, and brave. You make me smile. You do your best to protect me. And you have very nice arms."

That gets a reaction from him. The scowl leaves his face, replaced by a hint of a smile. "You would choose your mate based off of his arms?"

"*Oui*, especially when they are so nice."

He chuckles. "Because there are two of them?"

"Two is a bonus," I admit playfully. "You sound so skeptical that I can find you appealing. Why is that?"

Zennek sighs heavily, and for a moment I worry about his mood. His tail no longer flicks with agitation but is still. "I do not know what I am doing," he admits. "I have never taken a pleasure mate."

"Then it is a good thing you resonated to me, because I can show you what I like." And I give him a brilliant smile.

He blushes so easily, this one. I can tell he is blushing even as he gives me a reluctant smile back. "You are not like the other hoomans."

"*Non*?" I raise my arms up and study them. "Two of these." I pat my legs. "Two of these." I grab my breasts. "Two of these...a very nice pair, I admit," I say playfully, and then reach between my thighs once more. "And one very soft, very wet pussy. I think I am much like the other humans, *mon beau*."

His gaze drops to where my hand rests over my mound, and there is a hot, hungry look in his eyes that makes me shiver with need. "Your tongue is different," he murmurs. "You told me yourself."

"Ahhh. I am French. They are American. That is the difference. My world is full of so many people you cannot count them all. Sometimes they come from very different places and it makes them speak differently."

"Like different caves?"

So sweetly innocent for such a beautiful man. I do not think he can comprehend how many humans there are, since his tribe is not very big. "*Oui*, something like that." He nods, ducking his head, and the sight of that makes me tsk. "Why do you always look away from me? Do you not like the way I look? Am I ugly to you?"

"Never," he breathes, and looks at me again. I can tell it's an effort for him, because the look on his face is painfully shy.

"You can look at me," I tell him. "I will not embarrass you again, I promise." I smile at him and then carefully stroke a finger down the cleft of my pussy.

His gaze immediately goes there.

"You see? It is not so hard to look at me, is it?" I tease, sliding my finger through my wet folds. "Look at how wet I am for you. Have you ever seen such a thing, *mon beau*?"

He licks his lips, and it makes me even wetter. "No," he manages. "I have never seen such a thing."

I lift my hand and show him how wet my fingers are. The cold air makes them ice up almost immediately, ruining the fun. "If I come over to where you are, will you run away from me?"

Zennek stiffens. "I do not run from you."

"*Bon,* then we have no problem." I get to my feet, hitching my now-torn pants to my hips. I move to his side and sit down next to him. His nostrils flare, as if he is trying to discern my scent. I'm sitting incredibly close, testing him, I suppose. I want to see if he moves away again, my shy gentleman. When he does not, I touch a finger to his chin and lift his head so he cannot duck it.

I lean in and kiss each cheek in greeting. "That is how we say hello amongst my people."

He touches his cheek, surprised. "You put your mouths on each other?"

"Just a friendly kiss on the cheek," I reassure him. "No more than that."

Zennek watches me for a moment and then leans in. I remain perfectly still as he brushes his lips over my cheek and then the other. His skin against mine is all velvety warmth, and when he moves close I want to just pull him close and bury my face against him, he's so damned delicious.

"There," I whisper when he leans back slightly. "Now we are friends."

"Should we be friends...or should we be mates?" He moves in close again, and for a moment I think he's going to kiss me, but he only rubs his nose lightly against my cold one.

It's such a sweet, tender gesture that I ache all over. "We should be mates," I tell him, and cannot resist more teasing. "But you will have to kiss me in other places for that."

"Will you show me where you like it?" He lifts his hand and

lightly rubs his knuckles over my cheek, and I lean in to the caress.

"Of course."

He nuzzles my nose again, caressing my face. "Mar-lenn. I want to claim you as my mate..."

"But you do not know how to start?" I ask, breathless. "Shall I show you?"

Blue eyes full of scorching need meet mine. "Show me, yes. I want to learn how to please you."

How can a woman resist such a command?

9

ZENNEK

*M*ar-lenn is the most beautiful thing I have ever seen.

My mouth waters and I stare at her in hunger as she gazes up at me. Did I think her pale skin ugly a short time ago? Now it takes everything I have not to touch it, to feel her softness. Her boldness and playful attitude make me shy, but I also like it. I like that she is fierce about what she wants, and that she laughs often. I like that her eyes are merry as she smiles up at me, her khui singing with enthusiasm.

Truly, I am the luckiest hunter of all. My mate does not mind that I am shy as long as I look at her. She will teach me how to please her.

So I look. And I look. I will watch Mar-lenn until the suns rise and set once more if she will let me. I think I could watch her for days on end and never grow tired of her. I am fascinated with her tiny nose, the point of her small chin, the smoothness of her brow and how it moves with her expressions. And her mouth.

I am constantly fascinated by her pink, pink mouth. I do wonder about her tongue, though, and how it is different from the others. It makes no difference to me, of course. I do not care that it makes her speak hoo-man strangely. She is my mate and I will cherish her and all her differences.

She smiles at me and reaches for my braid. "Before we begin, may I loosen this?"

It is an odd request, but I nod. "Why?"

"Because your hair is very sexy and I wish to see it loose." Her newly blue eyes are full of eagerness, so I cannot see what this will harm. Sexy? Me? I am just Zennek, another hunter, quieter than most. But she smiles and reaches for the tie at the base of my braid and then tugs at the loops of my mane until it is loose and falling down my back. Mar-lenn tilts her head and studies me, and then pulls my mane forward, dragging it over one shoulder and my arm. "Là," she murmurs. "So thick and lovely. I like this long hair. Promise me you will never cut it short."

Like Aehako, who is too impatient to bother with a braid? I have contemplated it in the past, but now I am glad I did not. "If you like it, I will leave it long."

"I like it," she murmurs, dragging her fingers through it. She reaches up and runs her small hands over my scalp, shaking my mane free, and her touch sends a shiver down my spine and makes my cock grow impossibly harder. Even the smallest of touches have that effect on me, and I bite back my groan. I want her to feel free to touch me however—and whenever—she pleases.

So I remain very still, saying nothing.

Mar-lenn rubs a lock of my mane between two fingers—she has five of them, it seems—and then looks at me. "Yours feels very different from mine, for all that they are the same color. Do you want to touch mine?"

My hand flexes automatically. Touch her? I want to grab her and thrust my aching cock into her so hard that she screams with pleasure...I swallow hard at the mental image and reach one hand out to her mane hesitantly. I touch it gently, and when she takes my wrist and pushes my hand down on her head, I caress her with more boldness.

She is right; she is much softer than me. Her mane feels like the softest, longest fur I have ever touched. The strands are thin and fine and cling to my fingers, and I am fascinated. It smells good, too. All of her smells good. Beyond the strange scent of the pod she was in, there is a Mar-lenn scent, and I am growing quickly addicted to it. She watches me curiously, and I think she wants words. "Soft," I manage to tell her.

"*Oui*," she says with her strange tongue. "Soft." Then she wiggles her mobile brows at me. "I am soft all over. I will show you."

And she gestures at the neck of her heavy tunic.

My tongue immediately sticks to the roof of my mouth. She wants me to take it off of her? Or does she simply want me to caress her neck? I do not want her to be cold if I strip her leathers off, and I hesitate.

She puts her hand on mine, then guides my hand to her neck and the collar of her thick tunic. "Undress me, *mon amour*."

Her soft, sultry voice makes my sac draw up tight. My seed threatens to spill already, but I want to do as she asks. I want to please her. Eagerly, I tear at her tunic, ripping stitches as I pull the leather off of her.

Mar-lenn looks startled, but she chuckles. "That is one way to do it. Next time perhaps we use the ties so I have clothes to wear back to camp, *mon cher*."

"I will fix it for you," I tell her, panting. I will. I will not let her shiver in the cold. I cannot stop staring at her body, though. Now that I have torn her leathers off her, they hang from her shoulders and pool at her waist, but there is a long expanse of torso that is completely bare to my eyes. And I devour the sight of her.

Her teats are...magnificent. I have seen teats before, of course. Our females only cover them if they choose to, and a teat is exposed when a kit is hungry. But our people's are flat, only rounded with a bit of softness when engorged with milk. Mar-lenn has big, rounded teats that jut out from her torso. They look soft and bouncy and are tipped with pink nipples the same delicate color as her lips. As I stare at her teats, I see the tips harden, exposed to the cold. "Why are your teats so large?" I ask. "Is this normal?"

She chuckles, looking down at her chest. "Are they large to you?" She leans back and gives them a little shake. "It is pleasing to hear you say such a thing. They are just breasts, *mon amour*. Do you like them?"

I am fascinated by that little shake. They jiggle back and forth, and I cannot stop staring. "I...yes. I do like them." I glance up at her, noticing her skin prickling with bumps. "Are you cold?"

"*Un peu*. A little." Her eyes flare and she smiles at me. "Are you offering to keep me warm?"

I am warm. Of course. This makes sense. My khui singing so loud that it deafens me, I look around, then carefully ease Mar-lenn toward the cliff walls, where the wind is less likely to hit her. "Wait here. I will build a fire." Finding fuel should not be too difficult, and I carry the means of making a fire with me—

She grabs a handful of my mane, stopping me before I can get up. "*Mon beau*," she says softly. "I meant for you to warm me with your body."

"I see." I feel a little foolish for thinking of fire. Of course she means for me to warm her with my body. Mar-lenn holds her hands out, her playful smile on her face, and I pull her against me, wrapping my arms around her to share in my warmth.

I...am not prepared for what her body feels like against mine. Her teats with their tight little tips rub against my chest, and everywhere she is soft, soft, soft. And bare. I groan, nearly spurting my release as I realize she has no protective plating on her skin. She is just soft everywhere. "Mar-lenn..."

"I am here," she whispers, brushing my mane back from my face. "You are doing beautifully, *mon brave*." Her hands move across my jaw, caressing my face and then across my shoulder. "Are you well? You shudder."

Of course I shudder. She feels so good that I want to spill already. "I...fine."

My human mate makes a scoffing sound and then reaches down between us. "Do you need to come quickly so we can take time? I will help you with that, *mon beau*. Let me take care of you."

And then her hand is on my cock, caressing me through the too-thin leather of my loincloth. Shock echoes through my mind, and then hard, blistering need chases all my thoughts away. With a choked growl, I thrust into her small, soft hand. Once, twice, I pump against her touch, listening to her murmur sounds of encouragement as she leans in and licks my neck.

When her tongue touches my skin? It is too much. A low snarl erupts from my chest even as my cock unleashes a torrent of seed into my loincloth. I come.

And come.

And come so hard, even as she continues to stroke me with her hand. Stars flicker in front of my eyes and the blood rushes through my ears, deafening me to all but the sound of my khui. Every muscle in my body clenches with the force of my release, and hot seed floods past my loincloth and onto my thighs.

When I can breathe again, I press my brow to her smooth one as she nuzzles my nose. I am...embarrassed that my first time with my mate was not inside her. But she only licks the tip of my nose. "That was beautiful," Mar-lenn says, her voice soft with emotion, and absurdly enough, I am happy that I pleased her.

"I...came too quickly."

"*Oui*, that was the plan." She puts a hand on my chest and nudges me, indicating I should go backward into the snow. "Now we can go slow and take our time."

I like that thought. More than that, I like the sweet smile she is giving me, as if my pleasure was *her* pleasure, too. As if I have not disappointed her in the slightest. It makes me feel good. She does not mind that this is new to me. She will teach me how to pleasure her...and I will learn so well that I will make her come twice as hard as I just did.

I give her a hesitant smile, aware of the seed cooling on my groin. "I should...clean myself first."

"Do not take long, then," she tells me, and rips a scrap of her tunic off and offers it to me.

I take it and somehow get to my feet. My knees are strangely weak and it is hard —so hard—to walk a few feet away from her. But I do so, grabbing fresh snow and scrubbing at my groin until it stings with the chill. The cold is good, because it means I will last that much longer next time. I hate that my brother Pashov and my tribesmate Dagesh have gotten to the nearest hunter caves before I did. Mar-lenn should have a fire to keep her warm, and fresh water to drink, trail rations to eat. Instead, there is only snow and my body to keep her comfortable. She deserves better.

I will just have to work doubly hard to pleasure her to make up for the lack of comforts. With that thought in mind, I return to her, full of determination.

My khui breaks into a strong, insistent song as I return to her side. Even that small parting makes me realize how much I want her, and I pull her close and nuzzle her neck, breathing in her lovely scent. Her arms go around my neck and she caresses me, her fingers trailing over my shoulder. "Welcome back," she teases. She adores teasing, my female.

I adore that, too.

"I think you should kiss me," she says, wrapping her fingers in my hair as if holding me to her.

Kiss her? I do not know what she means...and then I recall what Vektal told us about the humans and how they like to press mouth to mouth. She put her mouth on mine earlier, in front of the others. She wants me to do so again? It seems an odd caress to me, but if it makes her happy, I do not wish to refuse. I quickly push my mouth against hers. "Like that?"

"For starters," she says, and slides her hand down the front of my chest again. I immediately think of how she fondled my cock and it jumps to life once more, growing achingly hard in an instant. But she only caresses my chest, running her fingers along the lines of my muscles and tracing the ridges of protective plating even as she leans in again. I push my mouth against hers once more, but this time when I pull back, she leans closer and nuzzles her lips gently against mine. The slide of them is...interesting. Her mouth is so soft and fascinating that I remain still, letting her take over. She brushes her lips over mine over and over again, as if the simple act of them touching gives her pleasure. I find it increasingly pleasant as the kisses go on, and when she starts to nip at my mouth with little bites, I groan.

I can see why Vektal is happy about this kissing.

10

ZENNEK

I part my lips to make it easier for her to nip at me...and her tongue slides against the seam of my mouth. A groan erupts from me and my hands clench against her. Did she...was that supposed to happen? But she makes a happy little sound, and then Mar-lenn tongues me again.

I remain utterly frozen, my cock throbbing in response to the slide of that smooth, wet tongue into my mouth. It feels different than my own tongue, but in a good way, and I do not know what about it makes her speak so differently. Because it is so smooth and slippery? If so, I welcome this, because her tongue rubbing up against mine...it makes my body react with fiery need.

She chuckles against my mouth and then bites gently at my lower lip. "Are you all right?"

"I like your tongue," I rasp out. "I do not care that it is strange."

That makes her pause. She draws back, studying me. "Strange?"

"You said you speak unlike the others because your tongue is different." I touch her face to comfort her. "This does not matter to me. I like you just as you are."

Mar-lenn stares at me, and then giggles. "Oh, *mon brave*, you are *incroyable*. How charming you are." She cups my face in her hands and locks her eyes with mine. "Does it bother you, then? To touch tongues with me?"

"No. I like it."

"Then you should use yours on me as well, my Zennek."

My cock jumps at the sound of my name on her lips. She wants me to kiss her back? To tongue her back? I can do that. I slip a hand behind her neck to hold her against me and gently brush my mouth over hers before teasing my tongue against the seam of her pink mouth. Her eyes close and she leans in to me, so beautiful that my heart aches with the sight of her. With a groan, I stroke my tongue into the hot well of her mouth, seeking out that smooth pink hoo-man tongue. I flick mine against hers, and when she rubs her tongue against mine, I feel it right down to my sac, and gasp in surprise.

Her arms go around my neck, and she continues to flick her tongue against mine, insisting that the kiss go on. I am all too happy to continue, and hold her body against my chest as I lick and flick at her mouth, trying to tease her with my tongue and please her as much as she pleases me.

By the time we pull apart, she is breathing hard, her teats pushing against my chest. She clings to me, and there is a soft, dazed look in her eyes. "You're very good at that."

Am I? The realization that I am making Mar-lenn soft-eyed and hungry with need is a pleasing one. I want to do more. With a growl, I capture her mouth again, slicking my tongue into hers and stroking deep into her hot mouth. As I do, I realize...this is like mating her, just in a different part of her body.

I shudder hard, struggling to control my need as desire explodes through me at the thought. I am mating my Mar-lenn's mouth with mine. And she accepts me eagerly each time, tasting at my tongue like I taste hers, caressing me, meeting me with hungry responses.

No male was *ever* so lucky.

My need for her grows overwhelming, and I push us forward, until she is on her back in the snow and I cover her with my larger body. She is small and fragile, so I prop my weight on my elbows to ensure I do not crush her with my bulk, and continue to claim her mouth with deeper, surer strokes.

Mar-lenn makes a little mewing sound and breaks the kiss, panting. She looks up at me with such need in her eyes that I bury my face against her neck, kissing her there and sucking on her skin with fervent desire.

Her hands go to my mane and she drags her fingers through it as I suck on her neck. "You are so different from me, but in good ways, *mon beau*. I like that tongue of yours. Ridges." She sighs. "I never thought you would have ridges but now I want that tongue everywhere."

Everywhere is exactly where I plan to taste her. I growl a low response, then lick at her collarbone, at her pale skin traced with blue veins. It reminds me of how very delicate she is, and when I see the bright red marks my attentions have left on her neck, I vow to be more careful. She is my mate, my everything—I must be mindful of how fragile she is. Gentler, I press more kisses along the front of her chest, where she has no protective plating at all. She wiggles underneath me, arching her back in encouragement as I go lower, and I brush my mouth between her prom-

inent teats. Her hands grip at my mane tightly and then she
steers me toward one pink peak. "Taste me here, my Zennek."

Again, she says my name like a caress and I groan, grinding my
hips against hers, unable to control myself.

She gives a throaty laugh and locks a leg around my hips, and I
immediately latch on with my tail, holding her in place. I want
her wrapped all around me. I want to bury myself so deep
inside her—

But she pushes my head toward her teat again and so I give the
pink tip a quick, efficient kiss.

I am not prepared for her response. Mar-lenn moans, arching up
to shove her teat at my mouth again, and I can feel her tremble. Is
this place more sensitive than others, then? Encouraged, I brush
my lips over the peak, exploring the texture of it with my lips. Her
skin is slightly different here, pebbled and textured, with a prominent nipple. I feel the urge to nip on it and suck as a kit would—
except I do not feel much like a kit right now. I feel like the most
powerful hunter in the world with my female writhing underneath me. Mar-lenn likes my touch, though, and I know she
would tell me if I did something wrong.

I hesitate for a moment, then give her nipple a hard, thorough
lick, the ridges on my tongue rasping against it.

The breath explodes from her in a near-sob. "Zennek. *Oui*, just
like that, *mon beau*."

I growl again, because her response is staggering. Licking her teat
makes her that needy? No wonder she has steered me here. I lap
at the peak again, enjoying how hard it is against my tongue, and
then I suck on it, flicking my tongue against the tip as I do.

Mar-lenn's cry of response and the arch of her hips against my
cock tell me this is good—very good—and I redouble my efforts.

All of my attention is now focused on the teat under my lips, and I kiss and caress, lick and nibble and gently bite, all to wring more gasping, wild pleasure out of my mate. I want to hear her cry my name out again in that shocked, intense way. She claws at my scalp, then at my back as I continue to tease her nipple, and then when I cannot stand it any longer, I move to the other teat and attack it with attention.

Her hips rock against me, over and over, and her little moans and cries eat away at my resolve. I grind my cock against the apex of her hips, dragging my hard length between her thighs. My loin-cloth is gone, but she replaced her leggings after exposing her cunt to me earlier, and I grow tired of grinding against the leather.

I want to feel that patch of fur against my skin. I want to feel all of her.

I reach between us and she makes an erotic sound in her throat. "Mar-lenn," I murmur, grasping at the seat of the leggings. My fingers brush against the curls of her cunt, and I want to expose them. I tug at the leggings, and when they do not move quickly enough for my liking, I give the leathers a hard, fierce rip. Seams burst and then I shove the remnants aside, pushing my length against the warm fur of her cunt.

"Oooh, Zennek," Mar-lenn says, her voice throaty. "Let me look at how big you are."

But the way she says my name...it is too perfect. I groan and thrust against her cunt, unable to help myself. My need is too hard, too intense. I cannot control myself. More than that, I don't want to. Mar-lenn said she wants all of me, and so I will give it to her. I thrust against the cradle of her thighs again, rubbing my length along her heat...and her slickness coats my cock.

I groan hard, my control shattering. I press my brow to hers and thrust again. Her arms go around me, her other leg moving to lock around my hips, and then I thrust and thrust as she murmurs words of encouragement, her hands moving over my arms and caressing me everywhere. I am lost in a haze of pleasure, the only things in my world the warmth of Mar-lenn's soft body against mine, the wetness of her cunt as I grind my length against it, and the insistent song of our khuis.

I come again, too fast. Of course it is too fast. I need to come inside her, not thrusting wildly against the textured fur of her cunt, but I shudder over her, holding her tight as I paint her cunt with my seed, spilling over her thighs and hips.

She has had no pleasure yet, and I have taken mine twice. When I can breathe again, I groan and drop my forehead to hers once more. "I am a poor mate for you."

"Why?" Mar-lenn touches my face, the look in her eyes soft and beautiful. "Do you think I do not enjoy seeing you come so hard? For me, your touch is exciting, just as exciting as watching you lose control. I like all of your pleasure, Zennek, and there are many hours before dawn. We have time to touch more, do we not?" Her smile is sweet.

I sit up and gather a handful of snow in my grip, holding it until it melts and warms, and then gently bathing some of my seed away from her thighs. Even the sight of that arouses me, my khui humming a constant reminder that we have not yet fulfilled resonance. "I wanted to make this perfect for you," I admit.

"And you will. So far I have no complaints," Mar-lenn says, taking another scrap from her demolished leathers and cleaning my seed off of her. As she sits up, her legs spread and I can see a peek of pink folds underneath the fur on her cunt, more enticing slickness, and a curious little nub enfolded at the top of her cunt.

The third nipple, I remember Vektal told us. The females like to be touched there.

"May I look at you?" Mar-lenn asks, distracting me as she closes her legs. "You are different than a human man and I want to see what is mine."

I am hers? I like that she says such things. I remain still as she gets on her knees, brushing the last scraps of her leathers off of her body. I have ruined all her clothing and I feel remorse.

I open my mouth to ask if she is cold, but then she takes one of the scraps and runs it over my half-erect cock, and hunger blisters through my mind again. It stirs to life even as she wipes my seed away, and traces a finger down my growing length. "More ridges here, *mon homme*? No wonder Georgie is all smiles when it comes to Vektal." She follows the line of a vein with a light touch, and impossibly, my sac fills tight with seed again. "But I must ask what this is."

And she touches my spur.

I pause. "It is...a spur? It is like your third nipple, I suppose."

Her brows draw together. "My what?"

My brow flushes. "Your...between your thighs."

Realization dawns on her face. "My clit?" She spreads her legs in the snow, wearing nothing but boots as she sits atop the remnants of her leathers and parts her folds brazenly. "This?" She circles a fingertip around the small nub, and I am fascinated by the wet gleam of her flesh.

I swallow hard, unable to tear my gaze away. "Yes. That."

"It is called a clit, or clitoris. And it is a pleasure center." She circles it again before lifting her wet finger to my lips. "Is yours thus?"

I shrug, because my spur is less sensitive than my cock, where I would rather be touched. But I will let her touch me anywhere if she wants. I capture her finger between my lips before she can pull it away and taste her.

And groan.

It is a saying among the hunters of my tribe that there is no taste quite like a resonance mate on your tongue. I always thought of it as mere bragging, those that have received the greatest of gifts merely rubbing our noses into it, or that they had been so struck by their mates that they no longer could speak of such things without bias. But with that small taste of Mar-lenn on my tongue, I know every word is true. There is nothing quite like her. It is musky and delicious, pleasing to all my senses, and that small taste sets my body aflame.

All I know is that I must have more.

"Mar-lenn," I murmur, even as I turn to her and put my hands on her hips. I am fascinated by those wickedly spread thighs, the hint of gleaming flesh underneath the curls. Just a taste of her has made my body go wild...what will it be like if I bury my mouth in her sweetness?

I am about to find out.

My female does not look at her hungering male with fear in her eyes. Not this one. She is not shy in the slightest. Instead, she spreads her legs with a sultry little smile. "You wish more, *mon brave*? Come and taste your lover." And she leans back on her elbows, her cunt a silent invitation.

Good. I throw myself onto my belly and push my face between her thighs, my tongue seeking out her heated slit.

She lets out a little gasp as my tongue finds her warmth, and then her legs clench slightly against me. She lets out a pleased, throaty sound, and one hand goes to the top of my head. "Touch me how you like," Mar-lenn whispers, unafraid of my ravenous hunger.

"I want to taste you everywhere," I manage between drags of my tongue over her soft folds. She is so pink here, so pink and wet and hot. "*Everywhere*, Mar-lenn."

"*Oui*," she breathes. "I am yours, Zennek." Her thighs quiver as my questing tongue flicks over her nipple—her clit. Through a haze of lust, I wonder if she liked that touch, so I look up at her, my mouth still buried between her thighs, as I push my tongue against her clit again.

I am fascinated when she tilts her head back, her eyelashes fluttering, as if my mouth on her is too much for her to handle. Her lips part, her breathing irregular. So I do it again. And again, rubbing one side and then the other as I watch her. I move my tongue in a circling motion, tracing the bud, and she gasps again, her legs clenching against my shoulders, and her short nails dig into my mane.

Ah. I have figured out what she likes, then.

With a growl, I circle her third nipple over and over again. She wriggles against me, her need perfuming the air, her cries of pleasure echoing against the cliffs. I can smell her cunt heating with more of her juices, so I move lower, seeking the source of all that delicious nectar. I tongue every drop from her channel, dipping in so I do not miss anything, and she squirms against me, her breathing erratic. I go back to her nipple, loving her responses, and wanting more of them. I want her to come as hard as I have. I want to see her lose control, to see her entire body quiver with her release. So I keep teasing her clit and watch her as I do. When she continues to moan and tremble against me but does not go over, I give her cunt a long, slow stroke of my tongue. "Guide me,"

I say, my breath fanning over her pink folds. "Tell me what you need."

"Finger," she pants, pressing down on my head. "Use your fingers, Zennek. Push into me."

I do as she asks immediately, gliding one fingertip through the folds of her cunt until I reach her entrance. I push inside and she cries out immediately. She tenses all around me, her cunt squeezing at my finger and I am fascinated...is this how she will feel around my cock? With a groan, I lean in and put my mouth to her third nipple again, even as I thrust into her with my finger.

She quakes all around me, gasping. "Zennek! Zennek! Don't stop!"

As if I could. I thrust my finger into her ferociously, pumping into her as if it were my cock and she were taking all of me into her heated depths. She feels so good, so tight, and I can feel her entire body shiver and shudder as I use my tongue on her third nipple. She clenches up tight and then her thighs are pressing against my ears, squeezing hard, and she is gasping, whispering nonsense sounds as she arches, writhing against me. Then, with a little cry, her cunt floods with new moisture and she shudders, her climax overtaking her. Fascinated, I drag my tongue over her folds, wanting to capture every bit of sweetness, and I keep lapping at her shuddering body until she pushes at my head, indicating I should move away. Reluctantly, I slide my finger from her wet warmth and immediately lick it clean. She tastes so incredible I want to put my mouth back there immediately, just so I can have more like the greedy male I am.

Mar-lenn sighs heavily and puts a hand to her brow. "Oh, *là*. I have never come so hard, *mon beau*." Dazed, she lets out a long breath and sighs, slowly sliding her legs back to the ground. "Come and lie beside me for a moment," she tells me.

I move next to her, pulling her close. She lies on the remnants of her clothing and cuddles up to me, tucking her face against my chest as she catches her breath. She is so lovely and soft that I cannot stop touching her. I stroke her arm, her side, her back, trying to ignore the insistent song of my khui and my even more insistent cock. She needs time to recover so we can continue. Resonance has not been fulfilled, but my heart feels...full.

This is what it is like to have a mate lie in my arms. I never thought to experience such joy, but here I am, with the most perfect female beside me, her taste on my tongue and her body next to mine. She will be there to welcome me home from long hunts—or go with me—and nights by the fire will no longer be lonely. Many turns of the moons from now...we will have a kit.

A rush of contentment mixes with my hungry need, and I press my mouth to her strange, smooth brow.

She smiles, wrapping her limbs around me. "Give me a moment to recover and we shall have more fun, *mon beau.*"

"Take as long as you need," I tell her. If she needs days to recover, I will patiently wait...as long as I can feast at her cunt and hear her cries. Already I want her hand on my head once more, pushing me down to the spot I most want to be at. I brush my knuckles over her cheek, the need to care for my mate urging me on. "Are you cold? Hungry?"

She burrows against me, shaking her head. "I am wonderful."

She is, I agree silently. Mar-lenn is everything I never thought to dream for myself. I gaze down at her, my heart full.

"Tell me about yourself," she whispers, reaching up to trace her fingers along my jaw. "Do you have family?"

"A large one," I say, unable to stop touching her. I rub my knuckles down her arm, then graze the side of one teat, wanting to tease the tips but telling myself to be patient. "My brother, Pashov, resonated just before we did. My other brother Salukh has not yet, I do not think. And I have a younger sister named Farli. You will meet her when we return home to the cave."

"Parents?"

I nod. "My father, Borran. My mother, Kemli. Both living. They will be very pleased to meet you." And shocked that their quiet son has resonated, I suspect. If ever a female were to resonate to one of us, I thought for sure it would be Salukh, who is as capable as he is broad.

I am fiercely glad I am the one her khui chose, though. I hold her closer to me, sliding a hand down to cup her bottom, my thumb stroking over the spot that her tail should be. "You? Do you leave family behind?"

"*Non,*" Mar-lenn says. "My father abandoned us when I was very young. I do not remember him. It was always me and my mother, but she died a few years ago. There is no one left for me back on Earth."

"Is that why you are so happy to be here? Why you do not cry like the others?"

She leans back and studies me, grinning. "What is there to cry over? I have claimed for myself the biggest, fiercest, handsomest man in the tribe."

"I am none of those things—"

"*Non?* You are in my eyes." Her hand slides down between us and caresses my erect cock. "You are definitely the most ready man in your tribe."

I groan, closing my eyes as she explores my length with her fingers, then curls them around my shaft. "I must wait."

"Wait for what?"

"For you to be ready," I manage.

"Touch me," she says. "Feel how ready I am."

So I do. I reach between us and touch her as she touches me, caressing her folds lightly before delving to graze at the core of her. She is very wet, just as she says, and I cannot resist pushing a finger into her heat once more, just to feel her ride it.

Mar-lenn moans and clutches me close as I pump into her tight cunt with my finger. She presses hot kisses to my mouth, her need feverish. "Give me your cock," she whispers, and I groan with need.

"Are you ready for this?" I ask. "I will wait to fulfill resonance if you wish—"

She puts her hand on me and strokes, hard. I hiss, the breath rushing between my teeth. Her response is obvious. She is tired of waiting, my impatient human.

I capture her mouth with mine and she meets my hungry kiss with her own equally needy reaction. I am not sure how humans mate, but when I roll her onto her back, she does not protest. Her legs go around my hips and when I settle my cock against her cunt, she arches up against me.

"*Oui*," she says. "*Oui*, Zennek."

We? Yes, we are a "we," I think. I like to hear her say that. "Together," I agree, and fit the head of my cock at her entrance, and then stroke home.

Mar-lenn lets out a little moan, her nails digging into my back. "You're so big," she breathes. "Give me a moment to adjust."

Pausing is a good idea. The feel of her clasping my cock so tightly, so deep inside her? I have never felt anything better, and my sac tightens, ready to pour fresh seed into her sleek depths. I have come hard twice already, but it is not enough. Never enough. Being inside Mar-lenn feels...exquisite. This is where I am meant to be. But I must wait. I cannot hurt my mate with my eagerness, so no matter how desperate I am to sink into her once again, I hold myself tightly in check.

Her hand strokes down my arm, and then she reaches up and caresses my face. "You are sweating, *mon beau*. Are you all right?"

It is difficult to control myself when instinct tells me to grab her hips and plow into her deep and hard, to rut myself until I explode. "I wait for you to be ready," I tell her tightly. "I will not fail you."

"Never," she says, voice soft. "You are the best of men." Her smaller body wriggles underneath mine, sending pleasure launching up my spine. "I think I have adjusted. You can move how you like." She caresses my face again and then moves her thumb over my lips, then dips it inside.

I nip at her finger and rock my hips against hers lightly. When she smiles encouragement at me, I pump into her again.

This time she sucks in a breath, her eyes going wide, and I freeze. "What is it?"

Mar-lenn moans, shifting her weight underneath me. As she does, she rubs up against my cock. "Your spur is...in a most convenient place." And she squirms again.

I do not feel with my spur as intensely as I do with my cock, but when I thrust again, I realize that it drags back and forth against her clit as I move. I shift so I press slightly to the side and thrust deep into her again.

She cries out, her legs clamping around me, her head going back. "Oh!"

A growl rises in my throat, but I swallow it, lest I scare my mate with how primal I am in this moment. I thrust into her again, and again, claiming her soft body with each firm stroke. She takes me, her cunt so tight, and it ripples in response to each motion, no matter how hard I pump. She loves all that I give her, and when I look down at her, watching as I pound into her, my mate's eyes are closed, her lips parted with wonder, her beautiful teats heaving with the force of my thrusts.

It is...perfection.

Mar-lenn cries out, her cunt tightening around me and her heels digging into my backside as another climax overtakes her. I roar my pleasure then, thrusting with claiming strokes as my own release overtakes me, and then I am filling her with my seed, spilling into her with endless stroke after endless stroke. She clings to me, even as I continue to push into her with the last of my strength.

Mine.

My resonance mate.

My Mar-lenn.

11

MARLENE

I wake up and gaze at the night sky. It is still full of stars, and my eyes automatically go to the smear of green high in the sky, the one shaped like a heart. My mother is saying hello, I think, and I say a silent hello back.

Then, a warm body pushes my thighs apart and a hot mouth covers my pussy. I moan as Zennek begins to tongue me with hot, frantic flicks of that glorious beast inside his mouth. I have never felt anything like the raspy ridges there...save for the wonderful ridges that line his cock.

Mon dieu, but the aliens here in this world are very blessed.

It takes me moments to come, and he licks me clean and then covers me with his weight, thrusting deep as he claims me. Zennek comes quickly that time, and I hold him tight to me as he fills me with even more seed, our khuis humming their song so loud that my chest feels as if it is vibrating with his need.

We fall asleep again, and a short time later, he wakes me up the same way. So it goes, over and over throughout the night, claiming after claiming until my muscles cramp up from overuse and I feel sticky everywhere with his seed. I am happy, though. Very happy, and when he wakes me again with his frantic mouth on my pussy once more? I think I am a very lucky woman.

I wake up again sometime after sunrise, the weak sunlight in my face. The first thing I notice is that it is quiet—almost too quiet. I sit up, confused, even as I reach behind me, looking for Zennek. He is right there, his warm weight against my body, his side pressed to my side. "Are you warm enough?" he asks.

"Why is it so quiet?" I ask, sitting up and touching my ear. It feels a bit like the quiet after a rock concert, when the parking lot is thunderous in its near-silence.

"Your khui," he tells me, sitting up as well. "Resonance has been fulfilled." And he ducks his head away, shy again in the morning light.

I touch my chest. "That did not take long."

"Sometimes it is fast," he agrees, doing something with his hands and a knife. Carving? Now? "We will still sing to one another, but it will not roar at us as it did last night."

He's right; my breast is humming in an almost polite tone, a gentle song compared to last night's thunder.

"So I am pregnant now?" I touch my belly. "You are certain?" When he nods, I consider this for a moment and then decide I will not stress or worry about being a mother just yet. I have many months of pregnancy before me, and Zennek will be at my side...I think. "So what happens with you and me?" I ask. "Do we remain together?"

Zennek goes still. He sets down his knife and I see he has several thick bone needles in hand. He strings sinew through the hole of one and then takes a piece of my shredded tunic and begins to sew it with big, ugly stitches.

He is not speaking, though, and that worries me.

"Zennek?"

"I will not keep you if you do not wish to stay with me." His jaw clenches, and he will not look me in the eye for all that his words are reasonable. "I will not trap you at my side."

"Do you want to be with me?" I ask, because I need to hear the words. "It is I who do not wish to trap you." I reach out and gently take the mangled bits of leather from his hands. "After all, I'm the one that seduced you, *mon amour*."

As I take the leather from him, he stares down at his hands and then captures mine before I can pull it away. "I want you, Marlenn," he says, voice husky and full of need. "In my eyes, you are my mate."

I beam at him. "*Bon*. We are in agreement."

The smile he gives me is pleased, but I can see the blush creeping up his brow. I smile back at him, and then I feel silly for just sitting in the snow, naked, as we smile back and forth at each other. I squeeze his hand and then move forward, crawling into his lap. He is warm and big, and his arms go around me, just as I'd hoped. His mouth presses against my shoulder, and he holds me close. This is nice. I take the sewing in hand and gaze at the seams, trying to see a pattern. I have sewn many times in the past, because I liked vintage clothing, which required alterations to fit my figure. I think I can do a better job with the sewing than my big alien with his enormous blue hands. "You and I will have to remember to talk," I say to him as I study the stitches. "Your people are not my people and we will probably have many misunderstandings for a while, but we can get through them if we talk to each other. *D'accord?*"

"You speak wise words," he says, and then asks, "Let me see your tongue?"

My tongue? I turn my head to look at him, curious. I can feel the hard length of his cock pressing against my backside from my seat in his lap, but I am not entirely sure if his question is sexual. But I stick my tongue out, humoring him.

He studies it with great interest, touching the tip and turning my head slightly as if he would examine all of it. After a moment, a hint of frustration crosses his face. "I cannot tell. How are you different from the others here?"

"Different?" I'm confused.

He nods. "I want to see if it is something the healer can fix."

My lips twitch. "We will have to talk more about French, you and I. Perhaps I did not explain it clear enough."

"Tell me. I wish to learn all about you." And he rests his chin on my shoulder, one big hand rubbing up and down my arm as if he can't stop petting me. Normally such a thing would feel invasive and pushy, but...I love it. I love his touch and I love how he snuggles me against him. So I chatter as I sew the pieces of my tunic back together again, explaining to him about France and Europe, and how it is across the sea from America. I tell him about languages and many different cultures. I'm not entirely sure he can grasp the scope of what I tell him, but he listens attentively anyhow as I piece my tunic and leggings back together.

"I will need *un soutien-gorge*," I tell him, studying my piecemeal tunic. "Something to hold the breasts so they do not jiggle." I demonstrate just how much I jiggle, and I love his blush.

"I will get you more leather when we return with the others," he tells me. "And more needles."

"*Parfait.*"

I dress even as Zennek stands behind me and nuzzles my neck, being a distraction. Once I am all covered in my furs, though, my stomach growls and I am reminded that we are out here in the wild with no supplies, and the others are probably wondering where we have gone. "I suppose we must leave soon, *non*? Return to the others?"

"They will be waiting for us," he agrees, but keeps kissing my neck. He seems to be in no rush, and that makes me smile. I caress his messy, wild hair, thinking I should braid it for him— mostly as an excuse to get my hands on him. "Do you want to bathe before we return?" he asks me, pulling me from my thoughts. "There is a hot stream nearby."

A hot stream? Of course, the smell of rotten eggs is still in the air, but I have been so...distracted by my Zennek that I forgot everything but him. "You brought soap?"

"No, but I can gather berries. They grow close to the stream."

Berries? I think for a moment this is another misunderstanding between us, but then I remember that his long, thick hair smells like fruit. "Very well. Lead the way."

He takes my hand and leads me out of our canyon, and back out into the drifting snow and icy breeze. He does not talk as we walk, perhaps growing shy once more, but his hand on mine is tight and possessive as he leads me along. We trudge up a hill, and as we do, I notice that despite the heavy snow and desolate landscape, there is greenery all around. There are distant pale trees that sway like tall feathers, and it seems that near every rock, a weedy-looking plant grows next to it, sheltering from the wind.

The cliffs are covered with snaky-looking vines and small bushes with curling, long needles, and there are rounded mounds in the snow. Zennek releases my hand and approaches one rounded mound, reaching in and shaking it, and revealing a deep green bush with spiky-looking leaves and curled edges. He brushes the leaves aside, and then makes an impatient sound. "Someone has gotten to this one already. Wait here." He points at another distant cluster and heads toward it, presumably to look for more berries.

I watch him go, fascinated by the tight sway of his ass. It is the tightest, roundest male butt I have ever seen, and there is something so appealing about the sight of it. *Là*, but he is a gorgeous man. I watch as his tail flicks back and forth, practically teasing that wondrous muscular butt, and when he bends over to shake the next bush, it is too much for a female such as myself. Hands flexing, I creep up behind him along the top of the hill, skirting wide so he does not see me, determined to put my hands on such deliciousness.

I am paying more attention to Zennek's fine ass than my own footing, though, and when one of my boots hits a shallow drift, there is no purchase. I stumble forward with a yelp, and then I am sliding down the side of the hill on my belly, then tumbling wildly in a sea of snow that cascades down with me. For a breathless moment, it feels as if I fall forever, and then I land at the bottom of the hill with a thump on my back, a splat of snow onto my face, and I stare up at the sky, dizzy.

The air is gone from my lungs, and for a moment, I think I am dead.

Dead, because I wanted to grab a fine blue ass and squeeze it.

I would laugh, except I can't breathe. A sound gurgles out of me, gasping, and I try to draw air back into my lungs even as I wipe snow from my face. I swipe it from my lashes and manage to laugh, then suck in a gasping breath. Dizzy, I focus on the clouds overhead. One fluffy one looks like a heart emerging from a puff of cloud.

I smile to myself.

A moment later, a wild groan erupts nearby, and then I am hauled out of the snow and clutched against a big blue chest. A frantic hand touches my face, sliding down my arms and legs, checking me over. He brushes over my side and I squirm, ticklish.

I giggle. "Is it playtime already, *mon beau*? I am ready." I reach up to touch his chest.

He growls and bats my hand away. "Where are you hurt? Is there pain?"

"I am just clumsy," I chide him, amused.

"I told you to stay put," Zennek says, his tone furious. "Not every step in the snow is safe. You have to be careful for hidden dangers masked by the snowfall."

"I have learned that the hard way, *non*?" I chuckle, wiggling my foot as he runs a hand down my boot. "But perhaps you should undress me and check me over anyhow." I'm getting turned on by all this touching, all this care. He clutches me against his chest as if I am the most precious thing in all the world and I adore it. I adore him...and I'm very aroused. His protectiveness brings out the fierce tigress in me.

Perhaps it is time I show my big blue lover what a blowjob feels like.

But Zennek frowns down at me, and when I try to touch his chest, he stops me, capturing my gloved hand. "Why are you laughing? This is not funny. Do you wish to die? Is that why you have no fear like the others?"

I laugh at his ridiculous words. Wish to die? Me? But my laughter dies in my throat when I see he is serious, his eyes full of worry and frustration. "It is not that I am afraid to die, Zennek. It is that I know I am safe." I point up at the cloud. "Do you see that?"

He looks up and then frowns back down at me. "A cloud?"

"*Oui*, but in the shape of a heart. That is how I know I am safe." I pat his chest and then reach up to cup his cheek. "I told you my mother had passed away before I came here, yes? She had cancer, a sickness that ate at her from the inside, and there was nothing the *docteurs* could do."

"*Docteurs*..." He tests the word on his mouth. "Healers?"

"Healers," I agree. Thinking of *Maman* and her last days always makes me feel slightly melancholy. "All my life it was just the two of us, and I was so sad that she was leaving me, but I was also terrified to be alone. *Maman* knew this. I would have no one when she passed. On her last night, I cried and cried and held her hand tightly, and she shook her head at me. 'Marlene, do not be afraid. I will always be with you. I will be at your side, always.'" *Marlène, n'ai pas peur. Je vais toujours être avec toi. Je vais être à tes côtés, toujours.* My breath catches in my throat with grief. "And then she was gone. The next day...I started to see the hearts. It was a joke between her and me, you see, that whenever we would part, hugs made her too sad. So we would make a heart with our hands." I lift both hands and put my fingers and thumbs together, making a heart shape as I hold them up. "It was a special thing just between us. I knew that when I saw a heart, she was at my side. I have seen them everywhere since she passed." I gesture up at the cloud, which looks even more like a heart now than it did moments ago. "And I know she is taking care of me. She is watching out for me and keeping me safe."

Zennek is quiet. He studies me for a long moment, and then nods.

His silence is distressing. I wanted him to understand, to realize why I feel so safe here even in this strange world, surrounded by aliens. "You think I am crazy, *non*? That I imagine things." For some reason, I am terribly disappointed.

But he shakes his head at me. "The spirit of your mother watches over you. I understand this. And it helps me understand why you do not scream and cry like the other females."

"I do not cry much," I admit to him. "*Mais non*, I am not afraid. I see many signs that this is exactly where I am supposed to be."

He touches my chin, then rubs one big, callused thumb over my lower lip. "Not exactly. Tell your *Maman* that I do not want you tumbling down any more hills. You are safest at my side, not at my feet."

I chuckle, relieved. "Understood. I will listen when you tell me to remain in one place next time and not be lured by your attractive body."

Zennek's brow flushes. "Hold onto me and we will go back to the stream and bathe."

I put my arms around my big alien's neck, holding on as he strides up the snowy hill with ease. I expect him to set me down when we return to the bushes, but he only snaps off a heavily berried branch, hands it to me, and then continues back down. We return to the small cleft in the hills, where the waters have worn the rocks down, and the smell of rotten eggs becomes almost overwhelming.

"Do you smell that?" he tells me. "That is a sign that the water is hot, but there is still danger here. You must always be careful when approaching a stream, because if the water is warm and appealing to us, it will also attract predators." Zennek sets me gently on my feet and then points at the banks. "Look for footprints and mud, signs that this is visited by animals."

I want to tell him that I have no plans on going out alone, but I nod. It's important for me to learn about this place if I am to live here with him. "Look for tracks. Got it."

"Do you see the reeds in the water?" When I nod, he touches my leather-covered arm, indicating I should stay in place, and approaches one. He leans in, grabs one reed, and then pulls it out of the water. On the far end is a creature—a fish?—that is more teeth than scales. It writhes and shudders, snapping its jaws as if trying to attack Zennek.

I gape, shocked.

"This is fang-fish. We sometimes call them face-eaters. They hide at the edges of the waters, waiting to latch on to creatures that drink. If you see the reeds, the waters are not safe. They will just as easily eat your face as that of a dvisti."

"What do we do?" I ask, watching as he puts the fish-thing back into the water. The reeds shudder with ripples, rearranging themselves as if to make room for the returning fish.

Zennek strides to my side, all masculine beauty, and I must be feeling resonance yet, because the sight of him makes me breathless. I want to grab him and lick him until his cock is wet with seed and then lick him all over again just because he is mine. I watch him with hot eyes as he takes the branch from me and plucks about half of the berries off of it.

"These are soapberries," he tells me, and crushes them in his hand. "They are good for cleaning, and good for chasing away the fang-fish. Watch." He returns to the water's edge and I force myself to stop paying attention to his fine ass and focus on what he's doing. He drips the berry juice into the water, and as I watch, the reeds immediately shiver and head upstream, trying to get away from the juice. He watches them, waiting for them all to leave, and then lowers his hand into the water and shakes it, cleaning it off. When that is done, he gets to his feet and looks back at me. "It is safe now. They will not return to this part of the stream until the suns are low in the sky. That is how you make it safe for bathing."

"*Bon*," I tell him, reaching for the collar of my leathers. "So it is safe to strip down now, then?"

Zennek nods, and immediately takes his loincloth off. The breath escapes my throat as I watch his male perfection. I love the sight of his heavy, nearly erect cock swaying against his thigh, thick with those pleasurable ridges that tore me apart in all the best ways. He has not noticed me staring, and squats by the bank, his tail flicking as he studies the water.

I strip off one layer, and then another as I approach him. It takes far too long for me to undress, but finally my bare skin prickles as the cold air hits. My nipples harden and goosebumps move up my arms, but I don't get in first. I wait, watching him.

When Zennek gets to his feet, he heads into the water up to his thighs, and then holds a hand out to me. I notice that his cock goes fully erect when he gazes at me, his eyes dropping to my pussy as if he remembers how he woke me up.

I certainly remember.

I ease into the water, somewhat nervous, but Zennek's hand is in mine and I know he would not let me get hurt. The water itself feels like a hot tub without bubbles, so warm that my skin gets

pink in response. "Oooh, *c'est bon*." This is amazing, and I immediately sink deeper, determined to immerse all of my body. At this
level, I am eye-height with his erection, and new, delicious ideas
form in my head.

He drops to his knees, hiding his glorious cock from my hungry
view, and I can see a blush at the base of his horns again. So shy,
my sweet Zennek. I chuckle and move to put my arms around his
neck, sliding my wet body against his. "Show me how to use the
soapberries then, my handsome mate?"

With a nod, Zennek strips a few more of them off the branch and
then holds them out to me. "Crush them in your hand to make a
pulp. It is good for the skin and mane."

I do, and lift my hand to my nose, sniffing. It smells like no soap I
have ever used before. Back home I was a fan of perfumed body
wash and shampoo, of course, but this is more like jelly than
soap. "Does it taste good?"

A hint of a smile quirks his mouth. "No, it tastes very, very bad.
You will vomit all day if you eat one."

Ew. "We will avoid that, then." Instead of cleansing myself, I press
my palm to his chest and begin to spread it across his delicious
blue muscles.

"I got the soapberries for you, my mate." There's an edge in his
tone that tells me he is growing shy again. Now that daylight has
come, it seems my Zennek forgets what a ferocious animal he was
last night as he claimed me—and how much I loved it.

"I know," I tell him. "And I am using my soap. Now let me wash
you." When he hesitates again, I continue, "It will give me great
pleasure."

That decides him. He relaxes, a small sigh on his lips as I soap
him up.

I'm not the most dedicated bath attendant. I soap his broad chest but I get too distracted by the lines of his muscles, the play of water across his velvet skin. I trace lines down his belly and then go to caress his cock under the water.

Zennek jumps at my touch, making a strangled sound. "This...is not bathing."

"Of course. How clumsy of me." I cluck at him, secretly enjoying the teasing. I soap my hands with fresh berries and then instruct him to wet his hair so I can wash it, making sure to dig my fingers against his scalp as I massage and cleanse. I keep my touches chaste, but he makes low groans under his breath and through the crystalline water, I can see the hard length of his cock jutting before him. He likes my touch, even if he will not allow himself to enjoy it just yet.

That's fine. It just gives me more time to tease.

As he rinses his hair in the water, I get more berries, crush them, and then begin to soap myself up. Wet hair first, which means I put both arms up and work my hair into a fruity, light lather. As I wash, I make sure that my breasts are high out of the water and pushing toward his face as I talk about small, chatty things. The bird singing nearby, the crisp wind, the sewing that I did earlier, the other survivors. Zennek tries to pay attention, but it is clear my bare, bouncy breasts—which I make sure to jiggle regularly—are distracting him.

I rinse, bending backward and making sure my breasts stay afloat. Then it is time to soap myself up, and I take a long, long time caressing my skin, moving over my belly and over my tits. I smooth soapy hands down my arms and make every gesture as erotic as I can. I pretend not to notice that he is breathing hard, my mate, or that he devours me with his eyes. Instead, I raise one foot delicately and place it on his shoulder that hovers just outside of the water. "May I use you to support me while I finish washing?" I even flutter my lashes to make my words seem innocent.

"Of course."

I anchor my foot against him and then stand up. My hips are now out of the water and he is seated in it, so I rise over him, my thighs spread. And I take more berries, crush them, and then wash my slippery, needy pussy, stroking fingers through my folds and teasing them as I do. He watches me with greedy eyes, and when I wobble, he puts a big hand on my hip to steady me. I thank him and pretend as if this is all normal and I'm not insane with need, then rinse myself.

"Oh no," I breathe, sliding a clean hand down my belly. "I think I missed a spot. Will you check for me?" I keep my expression innocent as I poke him with my toe.

Zennek growls, dragging me forward. "You are a tease, my mate."

"The worst of teases," I agree, my hands going to the arching horns on his brow. "Will you punish me?"

"Never." He presses a kiss to my belly, tender as ever. "Because that would be punishing myself."

I suck in a breath as his tongue grazes my navel and then moves higher. "Now who is the tease?"

He lifts his gaze to mine and gives me a hot stare that tells me exactly what he is thinking. "Are you sore?"

Oh, I am sore all right. I am sore because we both used each other so hard that I will have the most delightful bruises up and down my sensitive parts, but I do not care because it was so magnificent. He is magnificent. "I do ache," I tell him in a teasing voice. "Shall I show you where?"

"I can guess," he murmurs, dragging me lower into the water. I slide my legs down until I'm straddling his hips, and rock against the hard length of his cock. "You are a very obvious female."

"*Merci*."

That makes him stiffen and the desire leaves his gaze, followed by consternation. "Mercy? What is wrong?"

I frown at him, and then realize why he is confused. "That is not English, *mon amour*. French. *Merci* is thank you in my language."

He relaxes, his shoulders sagging. "I thought I had misunderstood you. That I was pressing you for too much."

Aw. My sweet alien. "I am a difficult female to misunderstand, my sweet." I keep my words English because I hate to see the worry in his gaze. "And you have not pressed me for too much at all. Am I not the one sliding her hands all over your large, wondrous body so you will drag me into your arms and ravish me?"

Zennek's eyes flare with heat again. "Is that what you are doing?" I nod, and he drags my hips down against him, settling the head of his cock at my slippery core. "Is this what my mate wants?"

I grind down against him, pushing at the head that teases me so deliciously. "Yes," I tell him, breathless. "That is exactly what I want."

His arm locks around my hips and he thrusts up into me, the movement hard and rough and forceful and delicious. I gasp, clinging to him, and his mouth finds mine. He claims me hard there, too, his tongue plunging into my mouth with a fierce claim even as he thrusts into me again, and my toes curl. I'm moaning and gasping against him as he jerks my hips down, pounding me onto his length. Last night he was tender and sweet but enthusiastic, but this is...rough, and I love it. I love all of it.

"Zennek," I moan as he drives into me, relentless. That teasing spur drags against my clit over and over, and I writhe against him, rolling my hips to try to get away from it because it is too much too fast, and I'm going to explode far too quickly if he doesn't stop. My moans become pants, my sounds turn to mindless mews of pleasure because he pins me against him and keeps pounding into me, over and over.

"My female," he rasps as he claims me. "My Mar-lenn. My wild mate. Is this what you wanted? Tell me." When I moan, he drives me down harder on his length. "Is this what you need? To be claimed this hard by your male? To have him take you and take you?"

"Yes," I cry, lost in his intensity as he fucks me so hard and says filthy things to me. My pussy clenches tight, and then I hold onto him for dear life as my orgasm bursts inside me, harder than I've ever come before, and every limb in my body seizes up in response.

He snarls low, then buries his face against my throat as he clenches me against him and his big body jerks with the force of his own release.

With a sigh, I cling to him, waiting for my thoughts to settle now that he has fucked them all out of my head. I am dimly aware of the warm water around us, his hand traveling down my back in a slow, steady caress, and the twitch of his big cock still inside me.

Zennek strokes a hand down my wet hair. "Did I hurt you? Just now?"

"Mmm, no. It was delicious." I lift my head so I can meet his eyes and smile at him. "We must do that again, and often."

He grins back at me. "Anything to please my mate."

And I love to hear that.

12

ZENNEK

When I can delay no longer, I guide Mar-lenn back to the ship and the others. Resonance has quieted for us, our khuis singing a gentle, contented song instead of the frantic one from last night. We must have taken right away. I have heard that some resonate for days on end, but it seems we are not so lucky. I am proud that she carries my kit so quickly, but part of me would have liked to stay alone together for several more days, just devouring one another with kisses and caresses until we could stand it no longer.

But we do not have the supplies for such a stay. I would have to take her farther out, much farther out to the next open hunter cave...and it seems smarter to take her back to the others where she can rejoin her people. She would probably rather be with them than a shy sa-khui hunter.

So we head back toward the campsite of the others. We get there to find it deserted, the torn-up snow and easy-to-follow trail making it obvious that they were headed to the Elders' cave.

When I tell Mar-lenn we must continue walking for a while longer, she does not complain. She just smiles at me and says one of her *fransh* words. I think she is agreeing, but her belly growls and I feel like the worst of mates. I have no food for her, no fire, and I continue to drag her along behind me in the cold. She does not protest, but I am angry at myself for not taking better care of her. I look around in frustration, and see a distant curl of smoke in the wrong direction.

A hunter cave, then. Someone has a fire. That will be Dagesh and his mate, hunkered down in a well-stocked cave. I watch that curl of smoke with a stab of resentment, and then grab Mar-lenn's hand.

My mate is bold, and I will try being so as well.

Mar-lenn follows me without protest as we double back a short distance, heading toward the hunter cave. I remember last night the sounds of Dagesh mating his human and how uncomfortably hard it made my cock. I have heard others mate in the past, of course. We live in a community cave and I have seen and heard everything. But last night it affected me in a way it never has before, because every time his human cried out with pleasure, I imagined my human doing so, and it made my cock incredibly hard.

I hope they are quiet this afternoon, or I will be spending the rest of the day trying to walk with a stiff cock.

It is quiet as we approach their cave, and I pause a short distance away, at the edge of the cliffs. The privacy screen is over the entrance of the cave, and it goes against all manners to ignore it, but my mate is at my side and her stomach growls fiercely with hunger. We will be with the others by tonight, but I do not want her to wait a moment longer.

"Stay here," I say to Mar-lenn, releasing her hand.

"Right here," she agrees, a smile playing on her lips. "This time I will not wander."

I give her a nod, and then because she looks so small and fragile, I give her a fierce kiss and then rush away. "I will not be long," I promise her, and head toward the hunter cave with determination.

Hunter caves are for all to use, I remind myself. They are stocked full of supplies by all because it is expected that one will have to stop in from time to time due to bad weather or simply because of a late day checking traps. Anyone caught in a storm can seek shelter in a hunter cave and know that they will be fine for days and days upon end.

Really, everything in that cave is mine as much as it is Dagesh's, I reason, and so I push the screen aside and enter.

Dagesh is in the furs with his mate, his female pinned underneath him. Her feet are on his shoulders and her face is bright red from exertion. They both hum with resonance, reminding me that my resonance mate is standing outside in the cold.

She gasps at the sight of me and pulls him down against her. "Dash!"

"Zennek," he growls, tugging the furs higher to cover his mate's pale body. "What are you doing? This cave is taken."

I look away, because I have no interest in them. "My mate needs food. I am taking some of your trail rations," I tell him, heading to the baskets at the back of the cave in the storage area.

The female makes a breathy noise, and I do not know if she is upset or aroused.

Dagesh just sighs at me. "Take it and get out. We are busy." And he moves over his mate, her sounds turning to ones of pleasure.

Even an intruder does not stop them in their mating. I can feel my face heating, and I dig through the baskets quickly, looking for what I need. There are trail rations, in a small leather pouch. I grab them and tuck it into my belt, and then see another basket, this one with leather strips and remnants, and a small sewing kit. I grab it, too, and a waterskin, then turn and leave.

Dagesh does not even acknowledge me with a grunt—he is too focused on his mate.

I return to mine, my belt heavy with my new prizes. Mar-lenn gives me a curious look, her brow wrinkling as she studies me. "Everything all right? I thought I heard voices."

"They sleep," I tell her, my face hot. "I woke them." It is only half an untruth—they were in bed after all.

"Should we go and say hello?" Her gaze searches mine.

"No," I tell her. "We leave them alone." I press the pouch of food into her hand. "Eat." I shake the waterskin and it is half full, so I hand it to her. "Drink. We still have farther to travel before we reach the others."

She takes a small bite, then coughs. "Spicy."

I give her a worried look. I did not stop to think if she could even eat what a sa-khui eats. Her teeth are different than mine...maybe her gut is, too? "This is bad? I can find a cache, thaw a kill for you—"

"It is fine, very fine," she tells me, and takes a sip, then offers me the waterskin. "But we will share, non?"

I drink, and when she holds a square of kah up to my mouth, it feels like a gift. I eat with relish, and like that she chuckles at my enthusiasm.

I wish I could stay out here with her forever.

FOR THE FIRST time in all my days, I am disappointed to see the Elders' cave. In the past, I have always viewed it as a fascinating place, one of old stories long forgotten and curious artifacts. Now, though, it is full of people when I would rather be alone with my Mar-lenn. The other humans receive her happily, and she kisses cheeks and hugs people, smiling back at them as Vektal gives me a nod of approval.

That nod makes me blush. I know he is pleased that my mate looks happy and that she is not scared, but he does not know Mar-lenn like I do. I have learned in the last day that my mate is many things, but timid and afraid are not on that list. She is easy-going and quick to laugh, and does not save room in her heart for worries. I will be the reluctant one in our pairing, I think, the one that pauses to consider all options. I do not mind this. I like my mate's boldness and I plan on encouraging it.

Thinking of all the ways I can encourage her boldness makes me blush again.

"You need to get the language," Vektal's mate says. Her name is Shorshie, and she already carries herself with an air of authority, steering my mate toward one end of the cave. "Everyone is getting the language before we leave. I promise it's painless."

"*Bon*," my mate says, and gives me a sly look. "Be gentle. It's my first time."

She winks at me as Shorshie snorts with laughter, and I bite back my own smile. Mar-lenn is deliberately trying to make me blush, I think. I like her teasing...and I plan to do some of my own when we are in private. I cannot be as flirty as her around the others, but I just smile back, because I will give as good as I get later. I think of how fiercely we mated in the stream, and how she demanded more with hungry little gasps even as I drove into her. She teased me because she wanted more mating. Is that what this is? If so, she will get it later tonight when we are alone once more. I vow to find a quiet place to sleep with my mate so I can lick her cunt until her teasing stops and her begging begins.

I like that thought very much.

Protective of my mate, I follow as Shorshie leads her toward the thing in the Elders' cave that shone a red light into my eye and gave me Mar-lenn's words. I watch, on alert, as my mate stands in place, unafraid, and waits for her turn, and when she collapses, I am there to catch her.

"She will be out for just a little while," Shorshie reassures me. "And then she'll be able to speak your language."

I touch my mate's face and look up at Shorshie and my chief. "Mar-lenn has more than one set of words, though." When they look at me with confusion, I add, "She speaks *fransh*. It has words I do not recognize."

Vektal looks to his mate, frowning, but Shorshie nods. "I can tell by her accent. Lots of humans speak different languages than mine."

"I want the *fransh* words," I tell them. "When she speaks any words, I want to be able to know them."

"If the computer has it," Shorshie says, and tilts her head, staring at the wall. "Do you, computer?"

"Please speak a few words of the language requested so I can identify it."

Shorsie looks at me blankly.

"Mercy," I remember. "As 'thank you'. And 'wee' as 'yes.'"

"Oh, I know a few words," Shorshie says, clapping her hands. "Moulin Rouge! Um, baguette? *Frère Jacques*?" She snaps her fingers and begins to sing nonsense words aloud.

"*Maman*," I add. "That is her mother's name."

"Language identified," the strange disembodied voice of the cave says. "Would you like to acquire the language 'Continental French'?"

I look at Shorshie and Vektal. "Would I?"

"That's it," Shorshie says, beaming. "Step right up."

I move forward, waiting for the Elders to give me the words of my mate so I can know all her thoughts.

I wake up with a pounding headache a short time later and immediately search for my mate. She lies on a pallet of furs, stretched out next to a few of the other females. I move to her side and curl up next to her, brushing her mane away from her brow as she sleeps. I slide my tail around one slim ankle, needing to be closer than close to her. Her khui thrums low, singing to mine as I hold her tight. I will not be easy until she opens her eyes and smiles at me once more.

Others come in and out of the Elders' cave. I see Aehako and Rokan, bringing in a fresh kill, and my brother Salukh is near the fire, talking gently to a few of the huddled females as he makes fresh tea. There is less fear on their faces today, but some of them still look quite unhappy. I am glad my Mar-lenn is of light spirits.

She stirs, groaning, and I rub my knuckles along her cheek. "This is worse than a hangover," she mutters, squinting one eye open at me.

"Hang...over?" I bite back despair—did I receive the wrong words? I do not recognize this one.

"It means my head splits as if I drank too much."

That I understand. "We have a tea that is good for headaches," I say, touching her face. "Shall I get you some?"

"Yes, thank you." She kisses my nose. "You are a good man."

I am an impatient man, I decide, because all I want to do is fling her down into the furs and see if I can get her ankles on my shoulders like Dagesh's mate's feet. But she hurts right now and she does not need me pawing her. I stroke her soft mane and force myself to get up.

I move toward the fire, watching my mate out of the corner of my eye. She gets to her feet, speaks with another female, and then heads behind a screen. Behind it, I know there is a pot for relieving herself. I still keep an eye on her location as I stand by my brother near the fire.

"Tea?" he asks. "For your mate?" And he holds a bone cup up to me. His cup, I notice, and for some reason I feel a stab of irritation. I will not let my mate drink from his cup. She will drink from mine and mine alone...but mine is not here.

I am being foolish. "Is it headache tea?"

He nods. "Heads are heavy with too many words this day. There are aching brows all around." He holds it out to me.

I take it, but my mate has stopped to talk to another female. They whisper, voices low, but my mate looks over at me and winks to let me know she is thinking of me. I will wait by the fire, then. I do not want her to feel crowded. Or...does she want me at her side? I do not know. This is my first time to be mated—pleasure or otherwise—and I doubt myself at every turn now that we are around the others. When we were alone and in the grips of resonance, it was easy. Lick her cunt. Claim her body. Make her wet. Wait for her sheath to clench with her release, and then take my own. Now, everything is different.

"What is it like?" Salukh asks, interrupting my thoughts.

I look over at him, confused. My thoughts are so full of Mar-lenn I have not been paying attention to my brother. "Eh?"

"What is it like? Resonance?"

It feels odd to have my capable, self-assured brother asking me about such things. I am the shy brother, the one no one thinks of first. "It is...not what I expected."

"Better?"

"In all ways," I admit. "She is perfect."

He looks over at my mate, who listens as another female talks excitedly. She smiles patiently, and then glances over at me and licks her lips in a blatant fashion.

My brother laughs. I blush.

"I did not expect you to resonate to one such as that, I admit," Salukh says. "I thought if a human resonated to you, it would be a quiet, timid one. Not one like that."

"She is very different from me," I agree. "But I like those differences. They are a good thing." My Mar-lenn is bold enough to lead in the furs when she needs, and gives me the confidence to take the lead from her. She does not look ashamed to be with me. If anything, she looks as if she wishes to get away from the other females and return to my side, which fills me with pride. Perhaps I do not need to be a fierce hunter anywhere around her except in our furs. I catch myself smiling and notice she smiles back.

"I am happy for you," Salukh says. "I have never seen you filled with such joy."

I do feel as if I have smiled more in the last day than I have in all of my life. But I look over at my brother and his expression is thoughtful as he glances at the humans near the fire. He did not resonate. Both Pashov and I did, but Salukh's khui remains silent. I put a hand on his shoulder. "I am sorry it did not happen for you, brother."

"It will, at some point," he says with a shrug. "Or it will not. At least now there is a chance." He gestures at the tea pouch hanging over the fire. "We need to set up a second pouch and make a stew for the humans. They will not eat their meat raw."

"No? But that is when it is juiciest."

He shrugs. "Humans have different ways of eating." I notice his tongue moves around their words easier, too. "Does your mate eat raw meat, then?"

"I do not know." I look over at her. "She has eaten kah but nothing else." I am suddenly filled with guilt that I do not know this simple answer. How do I not know what sort of meat my mate will eat? I want to rush to her side and ask her about this, but she is sitting with the females a short distance away, talking quietly to a teary-eyed one. She has my sewing kit out—she must have picked it up after she spoke with the others and threads a needle as she chats with the other female. Mar-lenn casts a smile in my direction, one that feels as if it is just for me.

"Come," Salukh says. "Help me butcher the dvisti that was brought back. Or are you going to stare at your mate all night and be useless?"

I bare my teeth at him. Duty to the tribe always comes first, especially if my mate is safe near the fire. I follow Salukh and get out my knife, ready to assist with the messy work of butchering a fresh kill. My brother's company makes the work go by fast, and I situate myself where I can watch my mate as I work. Salukh takes over the preparation of the meat while I scrape the gristle off of the hide, and as I work, I watch Mar-lenn.

My human mate is in the midst of the females, but I notice that she lets the others speak and she listens and observes. She participates, but I notice her head bends over her sewing and she talks to the crying one at her side more than any others.

Maybe my Mar-lenn is like me in that she is content to let others stand closest to the fire and take the lead. Perhaps we are not such an odd match after all.

Salukh elbows me, making my scraper skid across the hide. "You grin like a fool."

I snort. "You would too."

He grunts. "I suppose I would."

13

ZENNEK

*B*eing around the others again makes the night feel endless. The humans huddle by the fire, talking and drinking tea and eating bowl after bowl of a meaty, thick stew. Most seem content to pile together and chatter, and Mar-lenn is seated in the thick of them. I am too awkward to retrieve my mate, to boldly claim her from them and drag her to a private corner for touches. We will have privacy back at the cave, I tell myself, willing my body to be patient. We will claim one of the caves for ourselves, and set up a nest of thick furs so I can keep my mate warm as I devour her cunt all night long.

Until then, I will have to wait. She can talk with the humans around her, sharing stories and reassuring each other that all is well. I remind myself that this is new to them. They lean on one another because that is what is familiar. I give my mate space, going to her side occasionally to push a bowl of food into her hands to ensure she is well-fed, or to take her bone needles when the tips need sharpening.

Mar-lenn smiles at me and gives me gentle touches as I do, but does not get up from her spot with the human females, so I busy myself with other tasks. There are more hides to be scraped, and more kills brought in by the hunters. There are no signs of Pashov or Dagesh and their humans, which means their resonance has not yet been fulfilled, so we will all wait here in the spacious Elders' cave for them to return.

Zolaya squats next to me as I scrape a hide and watch my mate. "What is your female's name?"

A possessive blast rushes through me and I rock back on my heels, baring my teeth at him. "Why do you wish to know?" She is *my* mate.

He rubs his chest, and I realize he is resonating, and quite loudly. "Because she has been kind to my mate." He gives me a crooked smile. "Air-ee is very frightened and most of the females are impatient with her, but your mate is very kind and I can tell that it makes her comfortable. Will you thank her for me?"

I glance over, where my mate has been sitting with the same female. Their heads are together and Mar-lenn shows her the stitches in the leather she is sewing. She has sat by the same female all night, and I did not realize the weepy one was Zolaya's mate. "You resonated?"

He nods, his grin growing wider. "My heart overflows with joy. I did not know such happiness could exist." He touches his chest, rubbing over his khui. "I feel very lucky this day."

I sit back on my haunches and look over at my mate. I know just how he feels.

Mar-lenn looks up and her lips curl into a tiny, sly smile. Then, she raises an arm over her head and yawns widely.

I snort to myself, because my mate is not good at being subtle. I wipe my hands clean, giving her a challenging look.

She yawns again, putting away her sewing, and then toys with the neck of her tunic.

I know that hint, and my cock responds, growing hard instantly and pressing against the front of my loincloth. I rinse my hands with soapy water in a nearby bowl, and then wipe them clean once more as I rise to my feet. "I think my mate is tired."

"Tired of waiting, perhaps," Zolaya teases. "Go and find a quiet spot for the evening."

I can feel my face heat, but I think Zolaya is right. Mar-lenn rises to her feet as I move to her side, and I reach for her. "Come," I say, leaning in to whisper in her ear. "I know just the place."

"Someplace private?" She moves to my side, slipping her hand in mine.

I lead her toward where all the furs are laid out for sleeping. The female with the bad leg is already occupying one nest and Haeden lies in another on his back, pretending to relax. I move to one of the nests and roll all of the blankets up, then tuck it under my arm. *"Oui, très privée."*

Mar-lenn stops, her eyes going wide. She stares at me for a moment, and then moves closer to me. *"Est ce-que tu parles francais?"* You speak French?

"I had the cave give me your words," I tell her in her language. "I wanted to be able to hear everything you say."

Her hand flutters to her neck, and her eyes are curiously shiny. "I have never wanted a man as much as I want you in this moment," she says, her voice loud. "If you want me to drop to my knees right here and suck your cock, I will do so happily."

By the *ancestors*. Surely she jests.

I try not to look at my mate, glancing around the cave to see if anyone else has noticed Mar-lenn's bold speech. But they only look at us, puzzled. No one understood her.

No one except me.

I swallow the knot in my throat and speak up, using her language. "I plan on licking your cunt until you scream again. And again. At least twice, maybe three times. It depends on how good you are. And then I will mate you so hard that you will not be able to walk in the morning."

Mar-lenn gasps, and then gives a throaty little laugh. "I am so turned on right now."

"Then follow me," I say, ignoring the confused looks of the rest of the tribe as we speak nonsense words they cannot understand. I take my mate's hand and drag her after me, heading deeper into the Elders' Cave. "When I was a new hunter barely old enough to hold a spear, there was a place I would go to in here, hidden in the back. We will have privacy there."

"This is an old ship," Mar-lenn says as I lead her deeper into the cave. "Are these crew quarters?"

"I do not know what that is."

"Mmm. I suppose it doesn't matter. The only thing that matters is getting alone with you so I can rip that tiny loincloth off your magnificent cock and take it into my mouth."

I stagger, the furs spilling from my arms as her words paint a picture in my mind. *Again* she says such a thing. I look around, flushed, and then lean in, my voice dropping to a whisper. "You would take my cock into your mouth?"

She licks her lips, blatant. "You don't like that idea? But you licked my pussy last night. Several times."

"Of course. You are my mate. It is my pleasure to have the taste of your sweetness on my tongue." Even now, my mouth is watering to think about it. I am tempted to drop to my knees here in the long cave passageway and do so in this very moment, but I do not want someone else seeing.

"So I can do the same for you." She takes my hand again and picks up one of the furs, holding it back out to me. "It'll be fun."

Fun.

I cannot stop thinking of her suggestion. Of the hot feel of her mouth and tongue when she kisses me...what will that feel like if she sucks on me...a shudder ripples up my spine and my sac is tight, as if I am already dangerously close to spilling my release. I tug her hand and storm toward the cave I have in mind. It is one of the caves in the very back of the long corridor, with no flashing lights or anything inside it. It is just an empty cave, but the thing I have always liked about it is that the privacy screen built into the wall still slides forward if pushed hard enough, and I pull my mate into the room and tug the screen over the portal.

"A door," she says, delighted. "Marvelous."

"Yes, a door." I recognize the word in her language. I finish pushing it closed, leaving only a small gap wide enough for a finger to squeeze in, because once I closed myself in as a kit and only managed to work the screen—the door—back open again the next day. Ever since then, I have been careful in the Elders' Cave, but tonight, I do not much care about careful. All I care about is Mar-lenn and the hot promises she speaks of.

I toss the furs down on the hard floor and unfurl them, then look at my mate. She curls one lock of hair around her finger and bites her lip, smiling at me. So beautiful, my Mar-lenn...and so naughty. I point at the furs. "Lie down so I can taste your cunt."

"Mmm, so bold now that we are alone. I like it." She chuckles even as she completely ignores me. Instead, she moves to my front and puts her hands on my belt, tugging at the firm leather. "You didn't like my suggestion?" Mar-lenn looks up at me and licks her pink, pink lips. "I thought it would be fun."

"Mar-lenn," I pant, wanting to fling her down on the furs and rip her leathers off of her—again. "What you suggest...do mated couples do that?"

Her dark brows furrow. "Why would they not? You do it to me."

Why not, indeed. In all of my dreams of having a mate, of tasting her, holding her close...I never imagined such a thing. It feels like too much. "You truly want this?"

She licks her shiny mouth again and gives me a sultry smile, then pulls apart the knot that holds my belt in place. It slithers down my hips, my loincloth fluttering after it, and then I stand in front of her in nothing but my boots. My cock is already hard and aching, thrusting between us, and when I look down, I can see the head is beaded with droplets of seed.

Then, my wicked, naughty mate drops to her knees in front of me.

I groan, planting a hand on the cold, flat walls of the Elders' cave to steady myself.

"Look at this, you are too tall," she tells me, pouting up at me. She gestures at the distance between her face and my erection. "I need your cock at the level of my mouth. We shall have to think of something else."

Before I can even think, I drop to my knees in front of her. "Better?" I ask, voice husky.

She giggles, her pleased smile beautiful to see. One small hand pressed against my chest and she leans in. "Maybe you should lie on your back, my mate, so you can watch me better."

A sound of need rips from my throat, but I do as she commands —I am helpless to do otherwise. She could command me to run off of a cliff and I would gladly do so if she would only lick her pretty pink mouth again. I fling myself down on the furs and lie flat on my back, my cock pushing into the air as Mar-lenn watches me, undoing the laces at the neck of her tunic.

"Do you need to be naked for this?" I ask, curious.

"No, but it's more fun that way." Mar-lenn teases the neck of her tunic open and slides a finger between the deep valley of her teats, and I see what she means. I pant as I watch her, fascinated as she caresses her teats through the gap at the front of her tunic and then pulls the entire thing off over her head. Then they are revealed to me in their rounded glory, pale and tightly tipped, and I want to have one in my mouth. I groan, reaching for her, and she swats my hand away.

"*Non, mon cher*. It's my turn to have some fun. You lie back and tell me if I do anything you don't like." As I watch her, she pulls the tie loose from her braid and her soft hair cascades down one bare shoulder.

"I will like all of it," I blurt out. "You do not even have to touch me and I know that."

She bites her lip, amused. "Then perhaps you tell me which things you like the most."

And my beautiful, bold mate abruptly leans over and licks the head of my cock clean.

"That," I say immediately, my voice strangled. "I like that."

Mar-lenn giggles, pleased at my reaction. "Are you sure? Shall I do it again?"

I open my mouth to protest that I am positive that I liked it, but then I think of her hot tongue swiping over the head of my cock once more and close my mouth, nodding once. There is nothing that I want in this world more than her tongue on my cock again.

She leans over again, but instead of licking me, she gently blows on the wet head of my cock.

"I like that less," I point out, trying to be helpful. "Your tongue is better."

She laughs again, and the sound makes my cock jolt. "It is called being a tease, *mon beau.*"

"I like your teasing," I tell her seriously. "I like everything about you."

My mate sighs, looking over at me. "You really are the sweetest man. That deserves a reward of less teasing, I think." And she leans in close again, her soft mane spilling onto my thighs as she drags her tongue over the head of my cock once more.

I let out a strangled groan. "I like that," I whisper. "So much."

"*Bien,*" she says in a low purr, and then grasps the root of my cock as if to steady it, then swirls her tongue around the head once more. I watch, fascinated, my body humming with need as she licks the tip, then teases her lips over the head, toying with it, and with me. My bold mate then leans in further and licks me from tip to sac, her tongue moving over my ridges. She makes little sounds of pleasure as she explores my cock with her tongue, her hand going from the base of my cock to tease my sac.

I cannot breathe. She is too much, my mate, and I want nothing more than to watch this for the rest of my days, her pink mouth moving over the vein that runs down one side of my cock. She gives me a little squeeze, then leans over and takes my entire spur into her mouth, sucking and teasing the underside, rubbing it with her tongue.

I let out a fierce cry, my hands clenching into fists as I do my best not to spill into the fingers that tickle the base of my shaft.

"Shhh," Mar-lenn says as she lifts her mouth. "You will make them come running to see what cruel things the human female does to you."

"Not cruel," I whisper, panting. "Amazing."

She tongues my spur again—something I never thought sensitive until now—and then goes back to my cockhead. With another mischievous little smile, she takes the entire thing into the hot well of her mouth, stretching her lips wide as she sucks me in.

It is obscene.

It is beautiful.

I immediately lose control, grabbing a handful of her mane and holding her there as I pump furiously against her mouth. I shuttle against her tongue, barely pushing into her as I spill my release all over her lips and down her chin. I am both horrified and aroused at the sight of that—horrified that I have come all over her, and aroused at her wearing my release on her face. "Mar-lenn," I say, my arousal dying to shame as I realize what I have done. I came in her mouth, not her cunt. I got my release all over her face. "I am sorry—"

And then my bold mate licks her lips, her tongue swiping at my release. She tastes me and then wipes more off of her chin, feeding it into her mouth. "I wanted you to come quickly, *mon beau*. I like that I can make you lose your control like that." And she smiles sweetly at me, even with the spatters of my release on her face and breasts.

No male is worthy of such a perfect mate. My khui sings contentedly in my chest, as if in agreement, and I grab discarded leather —her tunic—and hastily swipe at the seed I have left dotting her pale skin. "I will get you something new to wear for tomorrow," I promise her. This tunic has had a rough time of it in the last day. Torn apart, stitched together, and now covered in seed. "Are you... well? Happy?"

She leans in and kisses me, and there is a strange taste on her lips. It is mine. I...am not sure I like tasting myself, but as long as it is on her mouth, I do not mind. She seems so pleased with herself, too. "I liked watching you," she tells me, no shyness in her at all.

I want to repay her. More than that, I want her taste on my lips. So when she moves to settle in next to me on the furs, I grab her leggings and carefully flip our bodies, rolling until she is on her back and I am over her. Her eyes flare with excitement, and when I tug her clothing down, she wiggles to help me free her. Her clothing gets stuck on her boots, and it feels like a lesson in patience as I take my time and undo lace after lace, until the leathers and the boots and all of the garments fall away from her. And then she is just Mar-lenn, naked and glorious and waiting for my mouth.

I push her thighs apart eagerly and lower my face to her cunt, not surprised to find her sultry with arousal. She enjoyed licking me just as much as I am going to enjoy licking her.

And I am going to wear her release, just like she wore mine. With that pleasant thought, I go to work on my mate's sweet cunt. Mar-lenn's cries fill the small cave, and she rocks against my face, holding onto my horns for support as I make her come at least twice before I pin my panting, eager mate under me and thrust home into her once more.

It is a long time before we sleep, but I do not think Mar-lenn minds.

I know I do not.

14

MARLENE

*T*he next few days are ones of ease and quiet. Now that we are in the ruins of the old ship—what the tribe calls the 'Elders' Cave', we are comfortable and there is plenty of room for all, so we wait here for the others that resonated to return. Nora resonated to a male named Dazhesh or Dayesh. I cannot say his name the same as the sa-khui do. Stacy resonated to Pashov, who is my mate's brother. And the loud, blonde Liz has been taken away by a sullen male by the name of Raahosh for resonance.

Zennek and I were the first to return, it seems. Once I find that out, I am a little disappointed. We could have stayed out longer? Had more privacy? But it is just as well—we have enough privacy in our little room at night in the back hall of the crumbling space-ship, and here we have food and a roof over our heads.

Nora returns the morning after we do, and she is all giggles and delight. She is a pleasant woman, with a sweet personality, and adores her new mate. He has dried all of her worried tears and now she smiles all day long.

I know how she feels, being so ridiculously happy for no reason. I should be miserable like the others that have not resonated. After all, I am on the same wintry planet they are on. I have no route home. I will be living in this caveman culture for the rest of my days like everyone else.

But...I have Zennek. I do not care how much ice is in this world, because I have Zennek's smiles and his blushes. I have a mate that is bashful around his tribe and turns into an absolute tiger the moment we are alone.

Let it snow all it wants.

Ariana—the nervous girl—resonated to a male named Zolaya, and while she likes him, it is clear she is not very comfortable in this place just yet. Where Nora makes bawdy jokes and giggles every time her new mate passes by, Ariana looks strained and uncomfortable. It is not because of her man, I think, but something else that troubles her. Sometimes she looks miserable and it pulls at my heart.

She needs a friend, and so I will be that friend for her.

Because there is much to be done to feed and clothe so many people, the men of the tribe are very busy. My Zennek gives me a kiss each morning and tells me what he must do that day—sometimes he goes hunting, sometimes he goes out on supply runs to look for herbs for a particular pain-deadening tea, or roots that will be good for the stew the humans eat. There are furs that must be scraped and prepared, more boots and cloaks and mittens to be made, and weapons to be sharpened. All of the tools here seem to be bone, and because bone dulls quickly, it must be sharpened over and over again before being discarded, just like my needles.

Zennek leaves my side frequently throughout the day, but he always returns and checks on me, stopping to make sure that I do not lack anything. His attentiveness is sweet, and to keep myself busy, I sit with the other women by the fire and work on sewing clothing for myself. I notice some of the other women are impatient with Ariana because she cries a lot, so I keep her close to me and show her how to sew. Together, we sit and make ourselves bras to stop our breasts from bouncing under our tunics, and the saddest leather panties with a drawstring. We laugh and laugh at our "granny" panties, and Ariana seems more at ease as time passes.

"I can't believe you're sewing already," Nora says, shivering next to the fire in a big fluffy fur blanket. Of all of us, she probably struggles with the cold the most and lurks by the fire. "We haven't been here very long, Marlene."

I shrug, working on a pair of leggings since mine have been shredded by my eager mate twice now and resemble nothing more than piecemeal scraps. "There is no *boutique de vêtements, n'est ce pas*? So I must learn if I wish to look like anything other than a furry bear." I push my needle through the thin leather, which has been so expertly worked that it feels as soft as butter and as thin as cloth. "There is much to learn, and for now I can do this."

"Sewing is definitely better than...that." Ariana nods over at the sa-khui men on the far side of the cave.

I look over, and my mate and hers—and another I do not recognize—are stripped to their loincloths as they work. Zennek is bent over a hide that is spread over the floor, up to his elbows in a greasy-looking sludge that he works into the skin itself. His braid dangles perilously close to the next handful of slop he rubs onto the skin, and I make a mental note not to put it in my mouth tonight when we are alone.

Zennek looks up and his mouth curves into a faint smile, and then he ducks his head again, bending industriously over the hide he is rubbing. Off to one side, the chief—Vektal—dismembers a larger creature that looks a bit like a shaggy pony—and Nora presses her fingers to her mouth, revolted. I cannot look away, fascinated, as Vektal cracks the skull and then carefully removes the brain.

"You know how they say you never want to see how the sausage is made?" Nora says in a faint voice. "I think I'm seeing how the sausage is made and it makes me want to be a vegetarian."

It's not my favorite to look at the butchering, either, but I force myself to shrug. "Harlow is a vegetarian, she says, but she has been eating meat. There are not enough plants here for such a thing. We must be practical."

"Don't you ever get upset over anything, Marlene?" Nora asks with a shake of her head. "You are way too chill."

Am I? I am trying to be wise about things. Georgie went through the worst with the others but immediately took charge because her life—and that of the rest of us—depended on her. She is brave and strong, and I am trying to be practical, that is all.

Besides, it is easy to be brave and strong when I have my wonderful Zennek. I feel safe with him around, and I know he will protect me. How can I be afraid? "If my biggest problem is that I must eat very, very fresh meat, then that is not so bad a problem, *non*?"

"It could be worse," Ariana says, squinting at her sewing. "I guess it could be bugs. Or snails."

"Mm, if there was butter, I would eat all your snails for you," I tell her, teasing. Americans are so fussy about the funniest things.

"There you go again," Nora says, chuckling. "Nothing worries you at all. I need whatever is in the water back in France."

I simply shake my head and bend over my sewing once more.

"So any idea on when Stacy will be back?" Nora asks, bored and obviously chatty. "She resonated to your mate's brother, right?"

She did. Zennek had mentioned Pashov was his brother. Salukh too. And he has a sister. And parents. And...*mon dieu*, I am suddenly going to be part of a big family. "*Oui*," I say distractedly. "They resonated."

"It'll be a big family reunion when you guys get back to the main cave then, huh?" She props her chin up on her hand and stares into the fire. "Having a big family like that to lean on will be nice. Dagesh's parents are dead, so it's just me and him, really."

"Mmm," I say, because her words have stirred an uneasiness in my belly. I have never had a big family. It has always been me and *Maman*, and when *Maman* passed, I flitted from place to place, visiting friends, doing my best to keep myself occupied.

I have never had a *family*. Not like that. But Zennek comes from a large one, and for some reason that makes me anxious. What if they don't like me? What if I am nothing but an odd human to them, and someone they do not like? What if they find me unpleasant?

What if they turn my Zennek against me?

Surely not.

I am worrying over nothing. I look around the cave, hoping for a sign from *ma mère* that all is well, but no hearts leap out to catch my eye.

And even though I tell myself I am being silly and it means nothing, I keep watching for hearts anyhow.

STACY AND PASHOV return two days later, and Zennek greets his brother with a big hug. Stacy gives me a timid smile. "Looks like you and I are going to be sisters."

"*Oui, une famille*," I say, leaning in to give her a kiss to each cheek. "I look forward to it."

She smiles brightly and we talk throughout the day, and I like her, a lot. She has a very nurturing spirit and she sneaks little glances at Pashov throughout the day that remind me of my own besotted gaze when Zennek is near.

That evening by the fire, though, the chief gets to his feet. "Almost all have returned, so we will pack up and go to the home cave in the morning. We will make sure all mated couples have private caves and everyone will have a warm place to stay. You will meet the rest of my people," he says to the humans. "And you will be home."

Home.

Funny. It does not feel like I am home.

I ponder these words as I snuggle close to my mate around the fire. It grows late and Zennek casts me heated looks that tell me he is quite ready to go to sleep, and so I fake a few yawns. He immediately leaps to his feet, blushing, and then pulls me behind him towards "our" quarters in the back of the ship. Once we are alone, he pulls me into his arms and we make love, slow and fierce, until we are both exhausted and sweaty, panting as we lie atop the furs. He caresses my cheek as I lean against his chest, listening to the gentle hum of our khuis together.

And I think about Vektal's words. *You will be home.*

"Do you think your family will like me?" I ask Zennek, curious.

He chuckles, brushing a bit of hair back from my shoulder. "Does it matter? Resonance chooses."

I sit up, frowning, because I don't like that answer. "It matters to me."

Zennek looks surprised at my response. "I did not mean to hurt your feelings, my mate. I only meant that it does not matter what they think. They will like you because my khui has chosen you." He reaches out to trace a finger down my arm. "Because I have chosen you."

"But you haven't," I protest, sitting up. I don't know why I'm making this an argument, but I'm unsettled. "You didn't choose me. Your khui did. Just because it chose doesn't mean that your family will like me. What if they hate me? What if they think I am funny looking? I'm human—they've never seen one, right?"

"They saw Shorshie."

Oh. "Even so, I don't look like her. And I don't look like you. What if your parents think your khui has chosen poorly?" I wring my hands. "What if they don't like me?" *Alors*, why do I care? Why does it matter so much that strangers like me?

"Mar-lenn," Zennek says, sitting up. He puts his hands on my arms, forcing me to look at him. "My parents will not know what to think when their quiet sons return home with mates, it is true. It is not something I have ever thought for myself, and I know Pashov is the same. Farli is the only unmated female in our tribe and she is our sister. We thought we would grow old alone. Having you at my side? Resonating to you? It is an impossible gift, and one I cherish. My parents will not care that you are human. They will see how happy you make me—and how happy Stay-see makes Pashov—and nothing else will matter."

His words make sense, and I nod, even though I can't quite shake the feeling of unease in my gut. I am good at being the companion to one person—first, *Maman* and now, Zennek. *Maman* was always a loner, too. What if I'm not good at being part of a big family? What if I disappoint everyone? "I just worry."

"Salukh has been kind to you, has he not?" Zennek encourages. When I nod, he continues. "My little sister Farli will be beside herself with joy to have two sisters. You worry over nothing, my mate."

I smile at him, trying to relax about this. Funny how being on a new planet at the edges of the universe isn't as scary as meeting my in-laws.

I'm able to hold off my anxiety as we travel the next day. It's overcast, the sunlight faint, and everything around us looks gray. People's moods are uncertain as we head toward our new "home" and I admit mine is, too. Zennek fusses over me, making sure my furs are bundled tight against my body and handing me more of the spicy trail rations to nibble on as we walk. He offers to carry me, but I shake my head—I want to be able to walk into my new home.

I try to picture what it's like living in a cave. It'll be dark, I think, and smoky, and probably claustrophobic. Is this what you wanted for me, *Maman*? I ask the universe, but I see no hearts this day. I have not seen them for a few days, and I worry that I've missed a subtle signal. What if Zennek is not what she wanted for me after all and I've misunderstood all this time?

My heart aches at the thought and I shake my head. That can't be right. Zennek is wonderful and perfect for me. I'm just worrying because there is suddenly nowhere else to go. The place we walk to will be our final stopping spot...forever.

Lost in thought, I look up in surprise when Zennek grabs my gloved hand and squeezes it. "We are here," he says softly. *Nous sommes arrivé.*

We are? I gaze where he points, and sure enough, there is an enormous cliff up ahead, cutting through the snow. A large, triangular cave mouth gapes open at us, and smoke curls in the sky. The others around us are starting to chatter with excitement, and someone is crying, again. Someone is always crying. My mouth goes dry and as I watch, people begin to stream out of the cave itself.

They are all tall and muscular, intimidating from a distance, but up close I can see they have smiles on their faces. There are a few women mixed with the tribe, but most are male. And as I watch, one hunter moves forward and hugs a tall woman and man who stand next to a skinny girl. Salukh, I realize.

Oh. Those must be my in-laws.

My stomach suddenly twists into a knot and my steps slow. I let others pass us as they surge toward the entrance of the cave, and there is laughter and greetings, and everyone seems to be hugging or welcoming a fragile-looking, confused human woman. Everyone is kind, I know. That is not the problem.

The problem is that it is clear they are a family. Not just Zennek and his parents, but this entire tribe—they are like one big family. And I am not good with family.

"It will be all right," Zennek reassures me, pulling me against him. He knows I worry. After all, what place do I have amongst such a close-knit group when I have always been a loner with my *Maman*?

There is a happy cry from one of the older females, and I look over to see Stacy being embraced by Zennek's mother. Stacy's sturdy and on the taller side, but in the woman's arms, she's practically swallowed. Pashov stands nearby, grinning.

"My Pashov and not Salukh?" the woman says.

"Zennek, too," Pashov adds, shooting a look at his brother, who hangs back with me.

The woman's face turns incredulous and she scans the crowd, looking for her other son.

I bristle automatically. Why do they all think Zennek is not worthy of resonating? Why do they all think Salukh should be first?

Zennek puts his arm around my shoulders, tugging me close. "Do not get offended, my mate." He presses his mouth to my brow, whispering. "It is only because I am the quietest, and Pashov is not much better. Salukh is the one other hunters look up to, the one who knows himself the best. We have always thought he would be the first—or only—in our family to resonate many turns from now when another female grew of age."

My grumpy response dies in my throat. *Many turns from now when another female grew of age.* I keep forgetting there were never any females for my handsome mate, and no hope for a mate or family. Of course he would never imagine himself as one to get a mate. I squeeze his hand tightly. "I am glad you are mine," I tell him in French. *Je suis contente que tu sois à moi.*

"I feel the same," he replies back, the words melodic despite his guttural accent. I love that he learned French just for me.

"Here they are, Mother!" The skinny girl races forward toward us, her eyes wide and excited as she skids to a halt a few paces away. She looks at me with open curiosity, her mouth parted as if she has just seen a unicorn.

I bite back a chuckle. This is obviously Zennek's young sister, and she has the features of a girl on the cusp of womanhood, her body slim and coltish, and her height towering over mine.

"*Bonjour,*" I tell her, slipping off my glove and holding out my hand since I know that cheek kisses will just make people uncomfortable.

She takes my hand in hers and gapes. "Four fingers and a thumb! And what a strange color! Humans are so funny." But she beams at me. "I am Farli, and Zennek is my brother."

I can't help but like her and her enthusiasm. "I am Marlene, and Zennek has told me much about you."

She stares at my mouth, and then leans back, fascinated. "Your tongue makes our words weird. It sounds different than when the other humans speak."

"It is because she is *fransh*," my Zennek says. "She is special."

I squeeze his hand, because that is a sweet thing to say, even if it is not correct. Being French does not make me special, but I like that I am special in his eyes.

Farli grabs at my lowered hand and drags me forward. "Come! My parents are excited to meet you! You will come and stay with us in our family cave now, yes?"

Zennek releases my hand, letting his excitable sister drag me forward, and there is no time to be nervous. He keeps a hand on my shoulder as Farli tugs me toward the waiting group. "No," he tells her. "Marlene and I resonated, and we will have our own cave to start our family."

"Awww," Farli groans.

And then we are in front of Zennek's parents. They are older than I expected, but he has told me that they resonated later in their years. His father looks just like an older version of my mate, with the same strong jaw, proud nose, and tilt to his horns. He gives me a patient smile and I see Pashov in that self-deprecating grin. Kemli—Zennek's mother—is of a height with her mate, and looks older than him. Her hair is nearly entirely gray and hangs down her back in one long braid. She has an ornately decorated tunic, the collar a thick half-circle made of quills of some kind in a fascinating, almost hypnotic pattern that makes her look like a queen. She has the bold features of the sa-khui, with a prominent nose and a pointy chin and sharp cheekbones. She doesn't smile, just studies me for a moment and she looks so fierce and disapproving that I feel my nerves flare again.

But then her mouth quirks up on one side, and she looks just like Zennek. "My new daughter," she says, her voice soft and warm. She holds her arms out for a hug.

I move closer, and as I do, I notice the decorations on her collar seem to change as I get closer, like an optical illusion. When I move in for the hug she offers, I suddenly see them.

Hearts. Each painted quill is held on with a little decorative stitch that looks like a heart. Hundreds of them.

And I burst into tears. For the first time since landing here—since even longer, really, I weep.

"There, there," Kemli says, stroking my hair. "It will not be bad here. You are part of our family now. We will take care of you."

"My mate?" Zennek's big hand is on my back as I cuddle against his mother. I can hear the worry in his voice, and I know it's because I am weeping for the first time since he's met me. He's always been impressed that I'm so strong and calm compared to some of the others, but the moment I meet his mother, I'm bawling like a baby. He has to be rattled.

It's just...the moment Kemli held her arms out to me, I realized that despite all my worrying about being part of a family, I had a mother again. And seeing those hearts on her tunic? It was like my own mother was given back to me.

LATE THAT NIGHT, I lie in a brand new bed of furs with Zennek, staring up at the ceiling of our new home. We have a cave of our own, right next door to his parents and their larger cave. Ours is small, but it's cozy. I expected to have dripping stalactites from the ceiling, but it's utterly smooth and high, so even the smoke doesn't sting my eyes too badly when we light a fire in the central firepit.

I shift on my side and put my cheek on Zennek's chest.

He holds me close. "Tired?"

"Not quite." I am exhausted, but my head is too full of whirling thoughts for me to relax into sleep. Even two rounds of intense sex with Zennek hasn't quite pushed them to the back of my mind. There is just so much to consider.

"Hungry?" he asks, and there is amusement in his voice. "I am sure there is a basket of dried food."

"Or three," I tease, chuckling. Kemli was so excited at Stacy and my arrival that she went overboard with her generosity. Our new cave is filled with extra furs, dried food, herbs, tools, weapons, and everything that Zennek's generous parents could think of to start us in our little "family," as if we are not just one cave away from them.

He chuckles, tracing the length of my spine with a fingertip. "My mother has always been very devoted. She did not resonate for many years, you know, and expected to go all her life with only a pleasure-mate. And then when she was older, she resonated to a male twenty-seven turns younger."

I think of Borran's lined face. He must not have been young himself when they resonated. "And so she buries everyone in dried food?" I ask, amused.

"She did not expect to have one kit, much less four, so yes, she buries us in affection." He chuckles. "I hope it will not bother you too much."

"Not at all." From what I can tell of Kemli so far, she's loving and fussy, but Farli is independent, so I don't think she will be smothering. "It'll be nice to have family again."

"You are home," he says simply, and holds me tighter against him, his arms around me.

I am. The realization is an odd one. After *Maman* died, I felt rootless and lonely, and like there was no safe spot for me anymore. I drifted from Paris to the States, visiting friends and looking for connections and finding nothing. Perhaps that is why I have never truly felt unsettled at finding myself on this cold planet full of aliens. Home is not a place, it is a *family,* and now I have Zennek, so my heart is complete.

I feel...utterly complete. Happy. Content. And it has only been days since I arrived.

"How long does it take to fall in love, do you think?" I ask him, curious. "Do you think it is too early to be in love?"

"In love?" He considers the words. "My people do not have a saying quite like that one. I understand the meaning, but it is not the same for us. Resonance chooses, we do not, but we show our devotion to each other in action and deed. And we have heart affections." He squeezes me against him. "You have my heart, Mar-lenn."

It makes sense. They do not declare things and expect them to be believed. They show the person they care for how they feel every day. "You have my heart too, Zennek." I press a kiss to his chest. "And you are my home."

"Always."

15

ZENNEK

Current Day

"*P*apa, my hair is in my eyes," Zalene says as she scampers at my side. "Fix it for me?"

"*Viens*," I tell her, slipping into the French tongue that my family uses when we are alone together. I know it makes my pretty mate happy to hear her words on my lips, and Zalene picks up little bits here and there, but she is not as fluent as we are. Mar-lenn and I have talked of taking her to the Elders' cave and seeing if the language can be given to her, but ever since the great earth-shake, the ma-sheens cannot be trusted. I would rather have my daughter safe.

She trots to my side, her tiny spear in her hand, and stands impatiently as I pull her silky mane back into its tiny tail. Zalene's mane is the color of mine but soft and slippery like Mar-lenn's and it falls out of the ties often when we go hunting. I fix the tail below her ear again and then release my daughter, and she races ahead of me toward the farthest of our traps. I smile as I move behind her, watching carefully. She is getting older now, my little one, and she is about the age that I was when I began to set my first traps with my brother Salukh watching over me. I have been letting her take the lead more and more, even though in my heart she still is the tiny creature with no teeth and a hand that curled around my finger when she was first born.

"Over here, Papa," Zalene bellows at me. "Come on! It's still alive!"

I jog to catch up, and see that the fat hopper in the trap struggles against its trapped leg, thrashing in place. Sometimes we arrive on the kills frozen in the trap, or sometimes they end up breaking their own necks. This one is alert, though, its leg gravely wounded. My daughter stands over it with her little spear and looks at me with impatience.

I crouch at her side and decide I will let her lead. "What will you do with it?" I ask, genuinely curious. Mar-lenn is not a huntress. She prefers to focus on her sewing and taking care of my parents, who have seemingly aged overnight. Some of the kits have been taking creatures in as pets, which is a human affection that has grown since my sister Farli took in her dvisti Chahm-pee. I still do not understand it myself—animals are food—and I wonder which way my Zalene will fall.

She leans over, studying the hopper as it writhes. "It is in great pain, Papa. It won't be able to use that leg anymore, and that means some other predator is just going to come along and eat him up. We should put him down and thank him for the gift of his meat and fur."

I smile at her. "Spoken like a brave, wise huntress. Do you wish to do it?"

Zalene looks at the animal, her little spear in hand, and then looks up at me. "Can you do it, Papa?"

It seems she is still my little one. I hug her close. "Of course. Watch closely so you can know how to take care of an animal painlessly when you are ready."

My daughter and I are so intent on our kill that the time passes without notice. I show her how to cut the throat cleanly, and then how to let the blood run out so it does not clot inside and ruin the taste of the meat. We set the trap up again, and then Zalene does the skinning while I watch and instruct.

When the first icy blast of snow hits my face, I am surprised at the bitterness of it. I look up in surprise, and the skies are dark and angry. A bitter wind blows in, and I realize that a furious brutal season snowstorm is about to take over us...and I am out here alone with my daughter.

She shivers as she scrapes the hide, busy at work, and I consider our options. We are a good afternoon's walk away from returning to the caves, at the farthest end of our spread-out trapping trail. There is no way we will return to the village in time to seek shelter. My Mar-lenn is going to be very worried when we do not return home this night. "Roll that up, little one," I tell Zalene. "A storm is coming in and we must seek shelter. Do you remember where the closest hunter cave is?"

My daughter does as I ask, but she is slow and unhurried as only a kit can be, and I end up taking it from her hands and finishing the job quickly, then get to my feet. I take her hand and pull her along with me. Instructing can wait. Already the storm blows in thick, ripping at our leathers and making each breath burn in my lungs. Storms are not unexpected in the brutal season, but I did not pay enough attention to the skies, focused instead on teaching my daughter.

By the time we make it to the closest hunter cave, I am carrying Zalene and the snow is so thick that I cannot see farther than a few paces ahead. It is only my familiarity with this area that ensures I do not get lost, and I breathe a sigh of relief as I set her down at the snow-filled entrance to the cave. "Let us push the snow out the entrance and then put the screen up, yes?" I tell her, my voice calm. I have been out in many storms before, but never with my young daughter.

"Can we do story spinning while we work, Papa? And play games? I spy and tic tac toe?"

"Of course." Anything to keep her occupied, because we might be here a while. I move toward the fire pit and get started.

16

MARLENE

I yawn, slowly waking up. I must have fallen asleep, because the coals in the fire are dead, and the hut is chilly inside. Shivering, I pull out my firemaking tools and get to work, sparking a flame and then adding tinder until it makes a small fire. I add fuel, and then when it looks as if it'll last for a while, I relax back. It's very quiet today...wait, no.

There's a dull roar in the distance that's so constant it drowns out all the regular village sounds. Curious, I wrap a fur around my shoulders and head out of the front of my hut.

Snow immediately dumps on my head.

Sputtering, I swipe it off of my face and turn around. The tent-like roof of my house is covered in a thick layer of snow that's fallen from the lip of the gorge above. As I watch, more of it falls in clumps, overflowing the ledge up above. I step aside, surprised.

Because of the way the canyon's protective lip is situated, we very rarely ever get snowfall down here. It must be storming hard above. The sliver of sky that I can see is a dark, angry gray and the roaring is the wind of what must be a blizzard.

I shiver to myself, thinking of the bad signs from earlier. *Tell me all is well, Maman.*

I return inside to my hut and bundle up, putting on my over-wraps and gloves. Once I'm bundled up, I head out of the village and toward the pulley to wait for my mate and kit to come in from their hunt. They will be cold and my little Zalene will be needing her mama. Another woman is waiting at the pulley, one with blonde curls and impressive height.

"*Salut*, Kate," I say, keeping a cheery note in my voice. "Is Harrec out on the hunt?"

There's a ferocious, kittenish growl and then Kate's kitten comes bounding out of the snow, all white fluff and teeth. The thing's only a few weeks old and already bigger than a dog, which worries me a little around the children, but she reassures me she's got him under control. Kate kneels down and puts her hands out, and the cat drops a slobber-covered object at her feet, steaming. It's a stuffed bird made out of leather, complete with flappy wings. She picks it up, shakes it, and then throws it once more and the kitten goes racing away with another growl. Kate grins at me. "Puff's learning to play fetch. He's so smart."

I chuckle, moving to her side. "Don't let Zalene see that cat has learned such a thing or she'll want one." I glance at the pulley, trying not to let my concern show. "Has anyone come in recently?"

Kate sighs. "No, and this weather has me worried. I was supposed to go with Harrec earlier, but morning sickness hit pretty hard and I stayed in. Now I wish I'd gone out with him, because at least we'd be together." She chews on her lip. "How do you handle it when Zennek's gone for days on end?"

"Poorly," I admit. "But sometimes it is easier than others." Today, it is not easy at all because my little Zalene is out with my mate. It is like my heart is coming out of my chest with how anxious I feel. Just Zennek alone would make me antsy, but both of the people I love most in the world? I won't be able to relax until they're home again.

Kate laughs, and then makes a sound of disgust. "Ah, crap, I think I stepped in something."

The back of my neck prickles. "Which foot?"

"Huh?"

I shrug, indicating the answer doesn't matter all that much, but I can scarcely breathe as she lifts her right foot and scowls at the bottom of her leather boot.

Right foot. Again.

Le chat, I remind myself. He is big and he will leave big droppings. It is not anything to be worried over. I say nothing as Summer and Claire approach, wrapped up in their furs, and then the three women chat idly while Kate plays fetch with her cat. I stare at the pulley, silently wishing for my mate and daughter to return so I can breathe.

Ereven returns first, and Claire peels off from the group. Then Warrek comes down the pulley with a fresh kill, his long hair frosted with ice. He gives Summer a quiet smile even as his mate begins a one-sided conversation.

Then it is just me and Kate again. The storm rages overhead, and

Kate is as silent as I am. When the pulley moves again, we both look up. Harrec jumps the last few feet, then tumbles to the ground and lies flat at Kate's feet, acting as if he's fallen.

She gives a wry snort-giggle. "Get up. You're the worst actor ever."

"I could be terribly injured," he protests, but he's grinning.

"Is that so?" Kate immediately tosses the steaming, wet leather bird onto his chest, and the cat pounces. Harrec groans, and then he wrestles with the cat while Kate leans over them. "Don't let him win this time," she advises her mate.

"Let him win? I do not let him anything," Harrec manages, panting as he wrestles the cat into a hold. Mr. Fluffypuff's eyes are bright and his tail flicking with excitement as Harrec holds him, locked against his chest. Then, it licks his face, making the hunter sputter and Kate giggle.

"He won this round," she tells Harrec, offering him a hand. "Again."

"I shall win the next one," Harrec says, setting the cat down. He takes Kate's hand and lets her help him up. He bounces to his feet, still full of energy, and shakes the snow loose from his clothes and hair. "Hard snow above. Hardest one I have seen in many turns."

Kate's smile becomes a little forced and she looks over at me, elbowing her mate.

Harrec gives me a sheepish grin. "I did not see Zennek, but I am sure he is fine. He is an excellent hunter."

I smile at him, hugging my furs to my chest. "*Oui*, I am not worried," I lie. I am terribly worried. "But thank you for letting me know."

"Do you want me to go and look for them?" Harrec asks. "I can put on warmer clothes and go back out, see if I can follow the trails before they get completely covered."

I consider it for a moment, but I know just as well as Harrec does that this weather is not safe for anyone to be out in. It will be impossible to see before long, and I can feel the temperature dropping by the minute. "*Non, merci.* You go home with your mate and your kit." I gesture at the cat, who's chewing on the leg of his boot.

"Are you sure?" Kate asks, but she holds onto Harrec's arm.

"Everything will be covered in snow before long," I tell them. "You could walk side by side and not see each other. I will wait. Zennek and Zalene will be home soon."

"Zalene is out there too?" Harrec rubs his jaw and turns back to the pulley. He looks at his mate, and then shakes his head. "Let me get a heavy cloak and I will go back up."

My heart clenches. "Are you sure?"

"It will be dark soon," Harrec says, his normally laughing manner gone. "If he is carrying a large kill and has Zalene with him, he might be moving slowly...if he is out there at all. I will do what I can. Give me but a moment." He pulls Kate close and kisses her, then races toward the village, the cat scampering at his heels.

"I'm sure everything's fine," Kate says again. "I'll wait here with you, though."

"It's cold," I tell her. "It's not necessary."

"Nonsense," she says with a smile, and then proceeds to keep up a one-sided conversation about pregnancy and morning sickness and the advice Georgie and Maylak have been giving her. Harrec races past, this time heavily bundled, kisses his mate again, and then goes back up the pulley while Kate tosses the bird to distract the cat once more. I only half listen to Kate, my gaze focused on the lift as I hope against hope that I'm going to see a pair of familiar, beloved faces on it next.

The lift thumps back to the ground a very short time later, and Harrec shakes himself off, completely covered in snow and his cloak iced up. "The weather is too bad to go out," he says, an apologetic look on his face. "I did not get far before I turned around. They are probably sitting warm in a hunter cave waiting for the snow to stop."

"Bien sûr. A hunter cave." I nod. "That must be it."

Harrec glances at Kate.

She shrugs her own cloak off and hands it to her mate, but he immediately tosses it back on her shoulders again, bundling her up. "Do you want to come have dinner with us, Marlene? I'm sure they'll be back in the morning."

I shake my head. "You go. I'll wait a bit longer just in case." When they look uncertain, I force myself to smile and make a shooing motion. "Go. Feed your furry child." I gesture at Mr. Fluffypuff, who is even now trying to gnaw Harrec's boot off of his foot. "Enjoy your evening. Like you said, they will be back very soon. I'll stay here just a bit longer and then go see Kemli and Borran."

They look reluctant to leave my side, but when Kate's teeth begin to chatter, Harrec frowns at his mate and escorts her to the village. I pull my furs tighter around me and stare up at the edge of the canyon, waiting. It's cold. Very cold. Each breath hurts to take, and I shield my mouth so the air is warmer by the time it goes into my lungs. I wait until the night falls, and it's so dark outside that I can barely see the hand in front of my face, and I feel as if I'll turn into a block of ice.

My mate is out there in this. My baby.

I know I can't stay out in this weather, though. It's too cold and I am no sa-khui...and even the sa-khui aren't out in this. I have to go inside. I trudge back to the village, numb with worry. I don't head back to my own hut, though, because it's empty. I think about going to visit Ariana, to pour my worry out on my friend's shoulder, but her new baby is crying. I head instead to Kemli and Borran's hut and scratch at the privacy screen with frozen fingers.

"Come inside," Borran calls.

"It's me," I tell them as I enter, shaking off my furs. My fingers tingle the moment I step into the warmth of the hut, and my feet feel like blocks of ice. My face hurts from the cold. "Zennek and Zalene haven't come home yet," I say bluntly. "May I sit with you for a while?"

Kemli gets up from her spot by the fire and clucks over me. "You are not the type to worry, my daughter. It is just a bad storm. Come and have some tea."

I sit next to Vadren, and by their fire, I feel a little silly. They don't look worried in the slightest. "Zalene is with him, though."

"She is a smart one, little Zalene," Kemli says, pulling out her herb pouch and heading for the fire. "Reminds me of my sweet Farli."

I smile at that, though Zalene doesn't look like Farli much at all. Farli was all elbows and knees when I met her, and developed into a willowy woman. My daughter is stout and sturdy, but I wouldn't change a thing on her. "My little *cocotte* is young to be hunting though."

"Her father is with her," Borran says, and Vadren nods. "He has been out in worse weather."

They nod, and I watch as Kemli mixes tea leaves with the hot water bubbling over the fire. "I just...I have seen bad omens today."

"Bad omens?" Kemli echoes.

I have never admitted to Zennek's parents that I look for signs from my mother, and that the lack of them today is troubling me. "*Oui.* My people think certain things are bad luck, and I have seen a lot of bad luck today." I hesitate, then add, "Normally I see signs of...good luck. And today there are none."

Kemli stirs the tea, and no one laughs at my ideas. Of course they don't. They don't know enough about humans to know what is normal for us and what isn't. And Kemli is calm and patient and kind—nothing like my own hotheaded mother, but a mother just the same. "And this is what worries you?" she asks, her voice understanding. "What will you do if you never get another sign?"

I frown. "What do you mean?"

She keeps stirring the tea, and I watch as the water bleeds to a dark, golden shade. Kemli likes her tea strong, and I wouldn't be surprised if she put something in it to calm me like Ariana likes in her tea. "I mean just that," Kemli says easily. "You said you look for signs of luck—of good things to happen. What if you never see another again? What will you do? Will you let that guide your life? Or will you make your own luck?"

Her words make me think. I never considered that. What if my mother never sends me another sign again? Will I feel like she really has abandoned me? I consider this. I would never think she stopped loving me, just that maybe she can't watch over me any longer. Is that something worth panicking over?

I don't know. I remain quiet as Kemli dips a bone cup into the tea and then hands it to me. "I just need them to be safe, *Maman*," I tell her. "Just...safe."

"I do too, my daughter."

17

ZENNEK

I rub my stinging eyes and poke at the fire, yawning. I did not sleep this night, listening to the storm howl and tending to the fire as my little one slept bundled in the furs. It has been a long evening, and I have burned at least six of the dung cakes, which tells me that it should be morning, but it is as black outside as ever, the wind drowning out my thoughts. I move to the screen, noticing the smoke clinging to the roof of the cave instead of seeping out. I touch the screen covering the cave entrance, and sure enough, snow leaks in from the edges. I push the screen aside and as I do, snow falls into the cave. The entrance has been completely covered, and I scoop some of the snow into a basket to melt for drinking water. The entrance will have to be dug out so we are not buried, which will be my task.

Which means it will be a while before I can sleep.

I go to work, using my hands to dig out a tunnel and then I keep digging. A quick look outside tells me that the snows—always plentiful this time of year—are deeper than ever. The cliffs themselves are coated, and I can see no plants at all, even the nearby bushes completely buried. Ah well, this is what hunter caves are for. I shake off as much snow as I can and then retreat back into the cave.

Zalene is awake, poking at the fire with a stick. She yawns at me, her mane sliding free from the twin tails that Mar-lenn made for her yesterday. "I'm hungry, Papa."

"Let us eat, then." I shake the snow out of my braid and move toward the fire. "We might be here for a while, my Zalene."

She frowns at me. "But I'm bored, Papa. I want to go home. I want to see *Maman* and *Grand-mère,* and my friends."

I want that, too. I hope my Mar-lenn is not too worried. I think of my beautiful mate, smiling to myself. She is probably still abed, enjoying having the furs to herself for a night, and then she will scold me for abandoning her for so long. She will say that she needs to make sure that I remember how much I enjoy being in her arms so I come back, and then show me exactly what she means.

Ah, my fierce, bold mate. I want to be home already.

I look over at my daughter, who seems to be all of me and nothing of her mother, and absently fix her mane's tails. "I cannot change the weather, little *cocotte*. We must wait it out. That is part of being a hunter. Your mama knows this. Now, think. What can you do to pass the time? What would a hunter do?"

She waits patiently as I finish tying her tails, and then looks at me. "Can we scrape hides?"

"Of course." She loves the messiness of tanning, because it is an excuse to get dirty.

Her eyes brighten. "Can we rub the brain mash into them to make them soft?"

"We can. Did you save your brains from your kill?"

She nods, pointing at the basket of offal from her hopper. It is by the door and frozen solid, but will thaw near the fire quickly enough.

"Can we make Mama something?" she asks. "So she won't be sad that we're gone?"

My heart warms. "We can make your *Maman* something, *oui*. But this skin will not be ready today if we rub the brain mash into it. That will take many days to cure. But there are other leathers here for hunters to use."

Zalene smiles at me, her expression sly and for a moment, I see her mother in her. "If the leathers are for other hunters to use, then we can use them, right, Papa?"

"Right." I chuckle.

FOR TWO DAYS, I burn through fuel as the storm rages outside. Cake after cake of slow-burning dvisti dung is placed onto the fire, and I count the remaining fuel with a worried look. There is enough for several more days, but I will need to replace it so another hunter is not left wanting. The more supplies we use, the more work there will be done to ready the cave for the next person, and that is work that will take me away from my mate.

I try not to think about what will happen if the storm continues for another handful of days. We are fine and have supplies. That is all I need to be concerned about.

Zalene flops onto the furs. "I'm bored, Papa."

"I know." There is little to do, trapped as we are. My weapons have been sharpened to deadly edges, my needles too. The herbs I gathered have been dried, and all the skins are curing. Zalene has been working on a tea pouch for her mother, but she tires of working on it all day, and I do not blame her. "Sometimes all a hunter can do is wait."

She rolls her eyes and makes an exasperated sound.

How well I know how that feels.

"PAPA, WAKE UP." Zalene's hushed voice rouses me from my sleep, as does the small hand shaking my knee.

I rub my eyes, exhausted. I have not slept for these three nights now, watching over my daughter. "I must have dozed by the fire."

"I kept it going," she says, and her eyes are worried. "But I wanted to tell you that it's quiet outside."

Quiet outside? That can only mean one of two things—that we are buried under the snow once more, or that the storm has stopped. I glance up at the ceiling of the cave, but there is a normal amount of smoke there, nothing dangerous. I look at the privacy screen, and sunlight edges through the top.

Relieved, I get to my feet. "I think it has stopped snowing."

"Does that mean we can go home?" Zalene asks. "I miss *Maman*."

I move the screen aside and heft myself onto the hard-packed snow at the entrance of the cave. Over the last few days, I have made a tunnel outward, and re-dug it again and again as it filled up. The snow atop it is loose but thin, which means the snowfall has stopped, and when I look around outside, I want to laugh.

The white landscape is almost completely flat. Here and there, jagged edges of rock stick up, and the cliffs look as if they have been chopped in half at the belly, they are so short. "Come and look, Zalene."

My daughter crawls out and sits next to me on the snow at the mouth of our tunnel. "It's so deep, Papa!"

I nod. "As deep as I am tall, I think."

"Past your horns, even!"

I chuckle. "Perhaps past them, too." I glance at my daughter. "You know what this means?"

She groans and flops back dramatically in the snow. "Snowshoes?"

"*Oui, des raquettes*. We will never get home if I have to dig you out after every step." And I reach over to tickle her.

Zalene giggles, her tail flicking as she rolls away from me. "Can we have *le petit déjeuner en premier?*"

"You can eat first," I agree. "But you must be ready to go quickly. We have a long walk home and do not want to be caught if the storm returns."

We chew on kah—trail rations—as we quickly craft our snow-shoes from the surplus of bones kept in the cave for such an occasion.

I have one strapped to my foot when I hear...something. I grab my spear, heading toward the entrance of our cave, and move cautiously into the tunnel dug out into the snow so I can see what it is making noise. In the distance, a dirty white patch of fur catches my eyes, and then another, followed by staring blue eyes and a long body that scratches at the snow, then straightens.

A metlak, and far too close to our cave.

I flick my daughter with my tail and put a finger to my lips, indicating silence. I watch the metlak, studying it. There are not many near our home village, unlike the caves we used to live in, and so this is a surprise to see. Perhaps it is lost, or perhaps it was moving to new hunting grounds when it got trapped in the storm. I can confront one metlak, chase it away, but I do not want it to scare Zalene. It might be best to wait for it to move on.

My heart sinks as I see another metlak move toward the first, picking at its filthy mane and then moving forward and digging at the snow. They are far enough away that they do not see us, but I mentally vow to build the fire higher so they will stay back.

Then, another metlak appears. And another. One with a kit clinging to a teat. Another one, a bulky male. A cold finger of worry moves down my spine.

I can scare off one, maybe two, but an entire clan of metlaks? It is not safe. I creep back inside the cave, careful not to make noise. They are a good distance away, but I must still remain alert and watchful. I put my knives into my belt and add more fuel to the fire. "Keep this burning and stay quiet," I tell my daughter in a low voice. "We are not going anywhere this day."

With wide eyes, she nods at me.

MARLENE

I thought I would lose my mind when it snowed for three days straight with no stopping. Everyone paused by my cave to reassure me that all is well, that Zennek and Zalene are simply hiding out in a hunter cave, waiting out the storm. After all, Aehako has been gone as well, and Kira is not worried. I tell myself this is true, and stay busy sewing and visiting Kemli and Borran, and spending time with Ariana and her new baby.

Then, the weather finally clears and I begin to wait all over again.

Aehako returns, a frozen dvisti carcass hauled behind him and full of stories of waiting in a cave for the weather to turn. Others go out to check traps and exclaim about how much new snow has fallen.

But Zennek doesn't return. He and Zalene are still gone.

Two days of perfect weather pass and my belly aches with worry. I see no signs from my mother, no indications that my loved ones are well. And I cannot think straight for fear that they might have come to harm.

That night, my hands tremble as I pace in my too silent hut. *Please, Maman. A sign. Any sign.* To encourage her spirit—if it is here—I move to my tallow bowl candles and light one, thinking of her. At home I would light a candle at the church for her after her death. I stare at the small flame, watching as it flickers. It is a waste of a candle, of course. I have to make the tallow ones myself and everything is effort, and now that I have used the candle for *ma mère*, I cannot use it for anything else.

Because that would be bad luck.

I stare at the flame, and suddenly I am angry. Angry at the weather, angry at my mother, angry at the world. Angry that my baby and my mate have been taken from me. I grab the candle bowl and fling it across the room. It crashes into the stone wall, the delicate bone bowl shattering and the tallow landing in a splat on my stone floor. The flame goes out.

I am tired of waiting to be gifted luck.

I am going to make my fucking *own* luck.

THE NEXT MORNING dawns clear and cold, and I put on my heaviest leathers and my sturdiest boots. I get out my snowshoes and strap them onto my pack, along with a waterskin of fresh water and a big bag of trail rations. I add a couple of Zalene's favorite cookies, because *I am going to find them.*

I head for Kemli and Borran's hut to let them know where I am going. Salukh will help me go look for his brother, I think.

To my surprise, Borran is bundling up in thick leathers as well, and Vadren has a cloak on. "I thought you might show up," Zennek's father says to me. "We are going with you."

My mouth falls open in surprise. "You are?"

"Of course." Borran moves to my side and gives me a smile, putting a hand on my shoulder. "We are family. You are not alone, Mar-lenn."

It is something I still struggle with. I blink back tears of gratitude. "*Merci.* Thank you."

Kemli bustles to my side, all energy this morning. She tucks an extra hood around my hair and then hands me a pouch of still-warm cookies, Zalene's favorite, from the pungent scent of them. "I will make a big hot meal for all of you," she says. "So when you come home, you can eat and relax."

Home. I smile at her through the tears springing to my eyes. "Thank you, *Maman.*"

She touches my cheek. "They know how to survive, my daughter. They will be all right."

"I know," I tell her, my voice hoarse. "I keep waiting for signs of luck, but...I am tired of waiting. I am making my own luck today."

"Good," Kemli says. "Go and bring them home."

18

ZENNEK

apa, are they ever going to leave?" Zalene touches my knee, her little voice full of quiet frustration.

I rub my burning eyes, and the lids feel as heavy as stones. "I do not know, my little one."

"I miss *Maman*," she says, her little lip wobbling, and I hug her close.

It has been a long handful of days. The metlaks—seventeen of them—have not left this area. They smell our fire, and perhaps our food, and so they hover just outside our cave, waiting. They know we are in here, but they do not know what to make of us. When they venture close, I can see that they are painfully thin, and they constantly dig at the cliff walls, looking for bits of vines to eat.

I think they have decided to wait us out, and the realization is a troubling one. We are low on fuel chips for our fire, and once they realize it is gone, they will grow bolder and bolder until they strike. I do not want to think of what will happen when they do.

Metlaks will eat anything, and the thought fills me with dread. I rub my brow, trying to think. My mind is foggy, and I have not slept since the storm. I cannot, because I have to watch over my Zalene. She is small and needs protecting, and if the fire should go out, I worry the metlaks would be in our cave in an instant.

If I could rest, perhaps I could form a plan to get us out of here, but I am beyond tired. I cannot think past the need to protect my little daughter.

"Papa," Zalene whispers again, tapping my knee.

"What is it?"

"You don't look good. Your eyes are all red and you have black shadows under them." She crawls into my lap and tucks her face against my neck, her horns poking at my jaw. "You're not sick, are you?"

"No, little one," I reassure her, rubbing her back. "Just tired."

"Then why don't you sleep?"

I can't hold back my heavy sigh. "I would like to, Zalene, but I must watch the cave entrance to make sure the metlaks do not come closer. I must keep the fire going as well. I must watch the skies. I must—"

Her little hand touches my chest, patting it. "I can do those things, Papa."

"No, Zalene—"

"I can do it, Papa," she reassures me. "I can sit right here and watch the outside. I can stir the fire so it doesn't die. I can help. And I can tell you if the metlaks move. I'll wake you up."

I rub my gritty, aching eyes again. "I do not know..."

"I'll sit right here next to you, Papa," she says eagerly, and demonstrates, moving next to me at the front of the entrance. "And I'll watch the metlaks ever so closely. If they move at all, I'll wake you up and you can take care of things." She beams at me, so enthusiastic.

And I am so very, very tired. Perhaps that is why I agree. "You will wake me if they move closer to the cave?"

"*Oui,* Papa."

"And if they do anything unusual?"

"*Oui.*"

"And if the fire starts to go out?"

She nods at me, all eagerness. "I can do it, Papa."

I am torn. She is so little yet, but I am exhausted and I know that soon we must leave this cave and head back to the village, and I will not be able to do it if I do not manage to sleep some.

I do not have much of a choice. I pat my daughter's head before leaning back against the cave wall. "I will just close my eyes for a moment..."

"I'll watch over you Papa," she promises, but I am already asleep.

"PAPA," Zalene whispers.

I jerk awake. It feels as if I have not slept for longer than a moment. "What?"

"*J'entends Maman.*"

I frown at her, trying to understand what she is saying. What does she mean, she hears her mother? But then…I hear it too. There is a loud screech in Mar-lenn's native French. *"Casse-toi! Cours, connard! Allez-vous en ou je vais vous casser les couilles!"*

My mate is here. I can scarcely believe this. As I get to my feet, pushing Zalene behind me protectively, I hear others calling out and yelling. I move forward, casting aside the screen over the cave entrance, and I see them.

My father, Borran.

My brother Salukh.

Vadren. And then my mate, my beautiful, fierce Mar-lenn. All of them carry torches and they wave them at the metlaks that have been squatting a short distance away from our cave, waiting to eat our food.

Of course my fierce Mar-lenn has come after me. She never lets anything stand in her way. A laughter of pure joy—and relief— bubbles up in my chest, and I grab Zalene's hand, stumbling as I come out of the cave and approach them.

Salukh moves to my side, scooping up my daughter in his arms even as his mouth twitches with amusement. Off to the side, Mar-lenn continues to shout obscenities at the metlaks, who scurry away from our fire and the noise she makes. "What is your mate saying?" my brother asks.

"Nothing polite," I tell him, and gaze at them with relief. "I am glad you came."

Mar-lenn marches to my side, torch held in her hand. Her eyes are ablaze and full of tears at the same time. "Are you all right?" Her hand trembles as she touches my cheek. "Zalene?"

"Fine," I reassure her. "Just pinned to one spot and unable to leave."

"Good," she declares, and grabs my braid, dragging my face down to hers for a hard, fierce kiss.

I can hear my father and the others chuckle.

"*Maman*," Zalene says, and then I take the torch from my mate's hands as she reaches for our daughter. Salukh hands her over, and then Mar-lenn kisses Zalene's face over and over, and she sobs with relief, holding onto our daughter and my leg, too.

"You scared your *Maman*," she tells Zalene between sniffed tears. "You and your Papa both."

"We were going to come back," Zalene says sweetly.

"Always," I agree, and then my legs grow seemingly weak. I stagger, my torch falling, and Vadren is there to hold me up.

"Zennek?" Mar-lenn cries, and then her hands move all over me, looking for injuries. "Where are you hurt?"

"Just tired," I admit.

"Papa hasn't slept the entire time," Zalene says excitedly. "His eyes look like holes, don't they *Maman*?"

"Here," Salukh says, and loops my arm over his shoulders. "Lean against me, brother. We need to get back to the village before night, and we've a long way to go."

"Yes, it is time to go home," I agree, and then topple over.

MARLENE

I kiss Zalene's little face over and over again as she sits in my lap. I could kiss her a hundred times and never grow tired of it. I cuddle her close and keep looking over at my mate, who sleeps in a nest of furs in his parents' hut. The healer has seen him and proclaimed that there is nothing wrong, just a need for sleep, and so he naps while I smother my little girl with kisses and Kemli fusses over all of us.

"*Maman*, stop," Zalene giggles, pushing at my face as I go in for another round of kisses.

"Never." I smooch her again, just because I'm her mother. "I am making up for all the kisses you missed while you were out with your father and I was here alone and scared."

"No need to be scared," she tells me, all authority. "I watched over Papa for you."

"Did you, now?" Even the arrogant way she says that is adorable. I tweak one of her little horns as Zennek stirs in the furs. "Go see *Grand-mère* and check on the food, hmm?"

She hops out of my lap but doesn't head right over to Kemli. Borran snags her instead, and she immediately sits on his knee while he tells her a story about the time he met a metlak as a boy. Vadren sits across from me at the fire, sewing fringe onto a hood that looks to be about Zalene's size, and in her kitchen area, I can hear Kemli chopping roots to go into a stew. Salukh returned home to get Tiffany and Lukti, who will be bringing along old Drenol. Stacy and her babies will come by too, judging by the amount of food Kemli is making. Everyone will be crowding into the hut tonight because they're family.

I don't mind it. We're spoiled by their love. I watch my daughter laughing in her *grand-père's* arms, and Kemli shakes her head at their actions. I didn't even have to ask them to go help me find Zennek this day—they were ready to go. Salukh carried him home when Zennek was too tired to walk. No one expected any less, because they are simply family, and family does that for one another.

I turn to my mate, to check him as he sleeps, and to my surprise, he is watching me, a relaxed smile on his mouth. He reaches for my hand and presses a kiss to my palm, and all the need and heat and worry feels as if it's going to explode out of me. I jerk to my feet and tug at his hand. "We need to go home," I announce to the others.

"You do?" Kemli asks. When she sees my face, her eyes go round. "Of course. Zalene, will you help *Grand-mère* with the chopping?"

"You can use my knife," Vadren offers, and Zalene practically flings herself off of Borran's lap at the offer. She scrambles to get the sheathed blade, and I'm pleased to see that she keeps it sheathed until she moves to stand next to Kemli at the countertop.

"Will you be back?" Borran asks, amused.

My mate's big hands clasp my shoulders before I can answer, and he nuzzles my neck. "Perhaps," is all he says, and I feel his tail curl around my boot. It's surprisingly demonstrative for my Zennek, and all it does is fuel the fire of need in my belly.

"We are just down the path," I say, hesitating. Part of me is burning with need for my mate, but part of me wants to grab my little girl again and never let her out of my sight once more.

"Bye, *Maman*," Zalene says without looking up, and chops a large hunk of root.

"*Partons*," Zennek murmurs in my ear, and that decides me. I grab his hand again and drag him behind me, heading out the door and down the path to our hut. I can hear Vadren and Borran laughing with amusement at us, but I don't care. I have my mate back. They understand the urgency racing through my body right now.

My Zennek is in my arms again and I plan on showing him just how I feel about that.

We get to our hut, and the fire is out again, the interior so cold I can see my breath puff before my face. I don't care. I continue to pull Zennek after me until we are before our furs, and I push him down toward the bed.

He falls backward onto the furs, a chuckle escaping. "I see you missed me, my mate?"

I don't respond. I can't say the words that describe how I feel, how lost and afraid and alone I felt, how terrified that I'd never see him again. I pounce on him instead, sliding my hips over his and leaning over his big body to kiss his mouth so fiercely our teeth clash.

Zennek groans against my lips. His hands clamp down on my hips and he grinds me against the hard length of his cock, driving between my legs.

"Now," I tell him in French. "Quick. I need you inside me, *mon couer*." I pull layers off of my body, tugging at the belted furs that hold the thick, warm clothing close to my skin. He grabs at my belt, too, loosening the knot of it and then flinging it aside.

A moment later, he rips the crotch of my leggings, just like he did in the days we first met, and it sends a hot surge of need through me. I lift up off of his hips and he tears his loincloth off, and then he thrusts deep into me.

I cry out, my fingers clenching against his chest. "Zennek!"

"Here," he growls out. "Right here inside your wet cunt." And he thrusts deep again, his spur dragging against my clit as he pumps into me. "Do you feel that? Me claiming you?"

"*Oui,*" I moan. "*Oui. Oui. Je t'aime*, Zennek," I tell him with every hard thrust into my body. "Love you. Love you."

His movements are savage as he pounds into me, our bodies locked in a primal embrace. Each thrust is as erratic as it is rough, but I love all of it. I love that he's taking me so damned hard, determined to drive all the fear and worry out of my body and leave me with nothing but a delicious release. The orgasm curls up through my spine, rising and building inside my body, and I welcome it.

"My bold little mate," he says, clenching my hips and grinding me down against him so the next thrust feels even deeper. "My fierce Mar-lenn. You came after me, didn't you? You needed your mate."

I come with a hard rush—and a burst of tears. All of the emotion of the last few days pours out of me with my release, and then it feels as if all of me is losing control. I'm sobbing as he expertly flips me over and drives into me, pushing deep even as he holds my jaw and whispers filthy words into my lips before kissing them.

He comes a moment later, shuddering over me, and then we grow quiet, no sound but his panting and my sniffling. Zennek holds me against him, practically smothering me with his heavy weight, but I like the feel of him there and don't complain. "I needed that," I tell him, and hate the hiccup that rises in my throat.

Zennek chuckles and kisses my jaw, my cheek, my nose, peppering his mouth over my skin in repeated little nips. "You were very worried and tense. I could feel it every time you touched me."

"I thought I lost everything," I confess. "Just like when *Maman* died. And all the signs were bad, over and over again, but I ignored them. Maybe I shouldn't have."

"We are here," he tells me, pressing a kiss to the tip of my nose. "Did I not bring back our fierce little daughter safe and whole?"

I smile at that, because Zalene did wonderfully for one so young. "She will be an amazing hunter," I admit. "And you took care of her. I knew you would. I just...I didn't know what to think."

He touches my cheek in a simple caress, and then begins to undo the laces on my tunic, exposing my neck so he can press kisses there as well. "I must leave for hunting sometimes, and the weather might be bad. It will keep us apart, but only for so long. I will always come back to you, my mate. You think I could leave your side forever? Impossible. I am not whole without you."

I run my hands along his beloved body, touching his head, his shoulders, caressing his horns. "I was being silly, was I not?"

"No," he tells me, and kisses even more skin as he exposes it. He moves lower, his cock sliding free from my body even as he pushes the furs aside and reveals my breasts. I am used to my Zennek's stamina after turns and turns of mating, and I know he needs to come twice before he must take a break, and that the first orgasm is only the start.

"I just...I thought *Maman* would watch over me like she normally does, but I have seen nothing for days." I shift on the furs. "Perhaps it is all just in my head after all."

Zennek is quiet. I moan when he teases my nipple with his tongue, rolling it gently and then licking it. "Shall I tell you something?"

"What?"

"When we were in our cave, I kept Zalene busy."

"Mmm." His mouth is doing wonderful things to my nipple, teasing the underside just how I like it.

"We played the games you have showed me—tic tac toe and I spy."

Two of his favorite pastimes for cold nights. Zalene loves to play both games with us, and I smile to think of them doing that together. "You're a good papa."

"Do not distract me," he says, chuckling as he kisses lower on my belly. "I am telling you this because it is important."

"Apologies." I'm not all that sorry, though. Talking after a round of violent reunion sex is just as important as the sex.

"We played I spy many, many times," he tells me, lapping at my navel and sending ticklish little sensations all through my body.

I laugh at the inflection in his voice. Zalene is at an age where a game is fun, but twenty rounds of the same game is even more fun, and it gets tiresome for a parent. I can tell it was an exhausting time for him. "My poor mate." I slide my fingers through his thick hair. "And what did you spy in such a small cave?"

He lifts his head, hovering over my pussy. "That is what I am trying to tell you, Mar-lenn. We played I spy and every time we played, I would see hearts."

My own heart clenches in surprise. "What?"

Zennek nods. "Zalene saw them, too. She pointed them out to me. One of the kah cakes was shaped like a heart. The stones we used for tic tac toe. There was even a heart shape in the rock of the cave itself. There were hearts in the snow. Hearts in the coals. Everywhere. And then Zalene worked on her hides, and she kept seeing hearts in the edges of every hide."

My eyes flood with tears. I manage to whisper, "What are you saying?"

"I am saying perhaps you had no signs from your *Maman* because she was with us, watching over us."

I choke back another little sob, this one of joy and wonder. He moves up to kiss me and I fling my arms around his neck, needing to just hold him close for a while. "You're not saying that just to please me?"

"I do not lie," he says, stroking my cheek. "It was Zalene who pointed them out to me. So do not worry, my mate. All is as it should be."

Perhaps he's right. Perhaps *Maman* has been silent this week because she was looking out for my mate and my little one. I'm filled with such painful love that I cry silent tears against his chest, sending a quiet thank you to my mother's spirit, and to any other spirits that might be listening.

Thank you for bringing my family back to me. Merci de m'avoir rapporter ma famille.

"You have my heart, my sweet Mar-lenn," Zennek tells me, wiping away my tears. "I love you."

"I love you, too," I whisper to him, and then put a hand atop his head, my mischievous side returning. "Now go lower and do your duty to your mate's pussy, because we do not have long before we have to return."

Zennek chuckles, letting me push on his head to lower him. "Ah, my mate. We have all night." He presses a kiss to my hip. "We have longer than that, as well. We have forever."

Perhaps we do.

THANK you for visiting Ice Planet Barbarians and the 'OG' original tribe with me! For the author's note and links on more books in this series, flip to the next page!

AUTHOR'S NOTE

Hello there!

Thank you for making it to the end of yet ANOTHER Ruby Dixon book. I know there are a bajillion authors out there and I sincerely appreciate each and every one of my readers. You guys make me keep going, and I mean that with all sincerity. If you weren't as enthusiastic about the dragons and barbarians as I am, I'd have hung up poor Ruby's hat long ago. :) So before I launch into anything else, I just want to say thanks. In a world full of Candy Crush (which is awesome) and *Desperate Housewives* (also awesome), I'm happy you chose to spend a few hours with me and the blue guys.

Marlene's story has been hanging around in the background for forever, hasn't it? When I originally wrote her in, she was a background character that was never going to get her own story. Dare I say it, she might have been a red shirt...aka, cannon fodder. I actually had plans once upon a time for a GREAT BIG PLAGUE to revisit and kill off a lot of the tribe, but as each story progressed and we saw more people get their happy ever afters, it became harder and harder for me to get rid of well...anyone. I liked seeing everyone happy. If I was a truly edgy author that wanted to make you sweat, I'd kill off more people...but everyone grieved at Eklan's death (including me) to the point that I abandoned that idea and revisited the concept of giving happy ever afters to everyone I'd neglected for a while.

So Ariana got a story. Marlene gets a story. Soon, Nora and Megan will get their own stories. So...yay no plague? :)

Another reason that I never tackled Marlene was that she was always so very settled in. I knew no big crazy events happened between her resonance and when they returned to the tribe, and I wasn't sure that was enough story for anyone...but there's something comforting about a nice, cozy little story about a man-eater of a heroine who seduces her big virginal barbarian, right? There doesn't have to be anything ground shaking. It just has to be fun to read. It's nice to revisit old friends and say hello, and that's what writing this book felt like. No cave-ins, no metlak uprisings, no plagues - just sweetness and sexy times.

I'll save the plagues for Icehome.

I'm kidding.

FOR REAL, I'M KIDDING. PLEASE DON'T SEND ME HATE MAIL. :)

(I just had a plague in Fireblood Dragons anyhow!)

Marlene's always been a very independent character to pin down, too. Zennek as well. Some people in the tribe, like Stacy or Maylak or Georgie, absolutely thrive on being around people and being in the thick of things. From the get-go, I knew Marlene wasn't like that. She's very much her own creature and does whatever-the-fuck-she-wants and doesn't much care if she says hello to the tribe that day or not. Zennek's shy, too, so that adds into part of why they keep to themselves. They're just...happiest with Marlene and Zennek. :)

Of course, there's also family. Extended family - mothers and brothers and sisters - are something I haven't played with too much as a tribe. After the big khui sickness (man, you can tell I really love me some plague, can't you?) fifteen ice planet years before the humans arrived, a huge chunk of the tribe died, leaving a lot of orphans and fragments of families. In addition, it's a hard place to live, so we already have families fractured from hunts gone bad or times that there were no healers to help out with severe injuries. Everyone's lost someone. But...Zennek has brothers AND a sister. Marlene just had her mother, and she's having to adjust to Zennek's large family, and I wanted to shine a light on that, too. It was fun to have them be part of the adventure!

(Speaking of, ahem, family dynamics, Vadren hanging out and joining Borran and Kemli in their furs? I wanted him to have a little happy, too. Like Marlene says, if everyone's happy, who cares if it's a little unusual? I actually really love the loose triad of them because it shows that love changes but there's always room in the heart for more.)

Also - Zennek. My blushing, sweet, thick Zennek. What a sweet-heart. I loved writing him - and his flustered dynamic with Marlene. I also loved that he was secretly a bit of a dirty talker and took charge once he got over his initial shyness. He quickly became one of my favorite heroes to write, and I hope you agree!

I've rattled on for a while now, so I'll wrap my character discussion with a French discussion. Gah. SO. MUCH. FRENCH. I've tried to only use just enough French that I hope it's clear in context what they're discussing. If not, I either restated it in the text or opted to have Marlene speak in English, because I don't want you to run out and have to get a translator just to read my book. I had some INCREDIBLE help with Marlene's story. Sophie L. — a reader and French teacher — offered to read through and correct me, and she did such an amazing job at helping me authenticate Marlene that I'm humbled at Sophie's awesomeness and now need to name a character after her or something. Sophie, thank you SO much. Any mistakes at this point are mine, of course. You can lead a horse to water, but you can't make it drink, and along the same lines, you can direct an author to correct her bad French, but you can't slap her hand away from the keyboard if she makes new mistakes. I hope everything reads all right. :)

(Thank you again, Sophie!!)

I know there is a lot of love and support for Icehome and after this visit at Croatoan, the next two books should be both Icehome, which means the broader story will be moving forward. Stay tuned! I have some fun stuff up my sleeve.

<3

Much love,

Ruby!

PS - If you love talking books and love Facebook groups, we have a Club Book Fort where myself, Alexa Riley, Ella Goode and Kati Wilde pop in and talk books of all kinds - ours and other people's. Please drop by and say hi!

CAST OF CHARACTERS

At Croatoan

Mated Couples and their kits

=======

Vektal (Vehk-tall) – The chief of the sa-khui. Mated to Georgie.

Georgie – Human woman (and unofficial leader of the human females). Has taken on a dual-leadership role with her mate. Currently pregnant with her third kit.

Talie (Tah-lee) – Their first daughter.

Vekka (Veh-kah) – Their second daughter.

=======

Maylak (May-lack) – Tribe healer. Mated to Kashrem.

Kashrem (Cash-rehm) - Her mate, also a leather-worker.

Esha (Esh-uh) – Their teenage daughter.

Makash (Muh-cash) — Their younger son.

———

Sevvah (Sev-uh) – Tribe elder, mother to Aehako, Rokan, and Sessah

Oshen (Aw-shen) – Tribe elder, her mate

Sessah (Ses-uh) - Their youngest son (currently at Icehome beach)

———

Ereven (Air-uh-ven) Hunter, mated to Claire.

Claire – Mated to Ereven

Erevair (Air-uh-vair) - Their first child, a son

Relvi (Rell-vee) – Their second child, a daughter

———

Liz – Raahosh's mate and huntress. Currently at Icehome beach.

Raahosh (Rah-hosh) – Her mate. A hunter and brother to Rukh. Currently at Icehome beach.

Raashel (Rah-shel) – Their daughter.

Aayla (Ay-lah) – Their second daughter

Ahsoka (Ah-so-kah) - Their third daughter.

———

Stacy – Mated to Pashov. Unofficial tribe cook.

Pashov (Pah-showv) – son of Kemli and Borran, brother to Farli, Zennek, and Salukh. Mate of Stacy. Currently at Icehome beach.

Pacy (Pay-see) – Their first son.

Tash (Tash) – Their second son.

———

Nora – Mate to Dagesh. Currently pregnant after a second resonance.

Dagesh (Dah-zhesh) (the g sound is swallowed) – Her mate. A hunter.

Anna & Elsa – Their twin daughters.

———

Harlow – Mate to Rukh. Once 'mechanic' to the Elders' Cave. Currently at Icehome beach.

Rukh (Rookh) – Former exile and loner. Original name Maarukh. (Mah-rookh). Brother to Raahosh. Mate to Harlow. Father to Rukhar. Currently at Icehome beach.

Rukhar (Roo-car) – Their son.

Daya (dye-uh) - Their daughter.

———

Megan – Mate to Cashol. Mother to Holvek. Pregnant.

Cashol (Cash-awl) – Mate to Megan. Hunter. Father to Holvek.

Holvek (Haul-vehk) – their son.

———

Marlene (Mar-lenn) – Human mate to Zennek. French.

Zennek (Zehn-eck) – Mate to Marlene. Father to Zalene. Brother to Pashov, Salukh, and Farli. Currently at Icehome beach.

Zalene (Zah-lenn) – daughter to Marlene and Zennek.

———

Ariana – Human female. Mate to Zolaya. Basic school 'teacher' to tribal kits.

Zolaya (Zoh-lay-uh) – Hunter and mate to Ariana. Father to Analay & Zoari.

Analay (Ah-nuh-lay) – Their son.

Zoari (Zoh-air-ee) - Their newborn daughter.

=====

Tiffany – Human female. Mated to Salukh. Tribal botanist.

Salukh (Sah-luke) – Hunter. Son of Kemli and Borran, brother to Farli, Zennek, and Pashov. Currently at Icehome beach.

Lukti (Lookh-tee) – Their son.

=====

Aehako (Eye-ha-koh) –Mate to Kira, father to Kae. Son of Sevvah and Oshen, brother to Rokan and Sessah.

Kira – Human woman, mate to Aehako, mother of Kae. Was the first to be abducted by aliens and wore an ear-translator for a long time. Recently re-resonated to her mate a 2nd time.

Kae (Ki –rhymes with 'fly') – Their daughter.

=====

Kemli (Kemm-lee) – Female elder, mother to Salukh, Pashov, Zennek, and Farli. Tribe herbalist.

Borran (Bore-awn) – Her mate, elder. Tribe brewer.

=====

Josie – Human woman. Mated to Haeden. Currently pregnant for a third time.

Haeden (Hi-den) – Hunter. Previously resonated to Zalah, but she died (along with his khui) in the khui-sickness before resonance could be completed. Now mated to Josie.

Joden (Joe-den) – Their first child, a son.

Joha (Joe-hah) – Their second child, a daughter.

=====

Rokan (Row-can) – Oldest son to Sevvah and Oshen. Brother to Aehako and Sessah. Adult male hunter. Now mated to Lila. Has 'sixth' sense.

Lila – Maddie's sister. Once hearing impaired, recently reacquired on *The Tranquil Lady* via med bay. Resonated to Rokan.

Rollan (Row-lun) – Their first child, a son.

Lola (nicknamed Lolo) - Their recently born daughter.

=====

Hassen (Hass-en) – Hunter. Previously exiled. Mated to Maddie. Currently at Icehome beach.

Maddie – Lila's sister. Found in second crash. Mated to Hassen.

Masan (Mah-senn) – Their son.

=====

Asha (Ah-shuh) – Mate to Hemalo. Mother to Hashala (deceased) and Shema.

Hemalo (Hee-muh-low) – Mate to Asha. Father to Hashala (deceased) and Shema.

Shema (Shee-muh) – Their daughter.

=====

Farli – (Far-lee) Adult daughter to Kemli and Borran. Her brothers are Salukh, Zennek, and Pashov. She has a pet dvisti named Chompy (Chahm-pee). Mated to Mardok. Pregnant. Currently at Icehome beach.

Mardok (Marr-dock) – Bron Mardok Vendasi, from the planet Ubeduc VII. Arrived on *The Tranquil Lady*. Mechanic and ex-soldier. Resonated to Farli and elected to stay behind with the tribe. Currently at Icehome beach.

======

Bek – (Behk) – Hunter. Brother to Maylak. Mated to Elly.

Elly – Former human slave. Kidnapped at a very young age and has spent much of life in a cage or enslaved. First to resonate amongst the former slaves brought to Not-Hoth. Mated to Bek. Pregnant.

======

Harrec (Hair-ek) – Hunter. Squeamish. Also a tease. Recently resonated to Kate.

Kate – Human female. Extremely tall & strong, with white-blonde curly hair. Recently resonated to Harrec. Pregnant.

Mr. Fluffypuff aka Puff/Poof - Her orphaned snowcat kitten.

======

Warrek (War-ehk) – Tribal hunter and teacher. Son to Eklan (now deceased). Resonated to Summer.

Summer – Human female. Tends to ramble in speech when nervous. Chess aficionado. Recently resonated to Warrek.

======

Taushen (Tow – rhymes with cow – shen) – Hunter. Recently

mated to Brooke. Experiencing a happiness renaissance. Currently at Icehome beach.

Brooke – Human female with fading pink hair. Former hairdresser, fond of braiding the hair of anyone that walks close enough. Mated to Taushen and recently pregnant. Currently at Icehome beach.

———

Vaza (Vaw-zhuh) – Widower and elder. Loves to creep on the ladies. Currently pleasure-mated with Gail and at Icehome beach. Adopted father to Z'hren.

Gail – Divorced older human woman. Had a son back on Earth (deceased). Approx fiftyish in age. Pleasure-mated with Vaza, adopted mother to Z'hren.

Unmated Elders

———

Drayan (Dry-ann) – Elder.

Drenol (Dree-nowl) – Elder. Friend to Lukti.

Vadren (Vaw-dren) – Elder. Sometimes bedmate to Kemli and Borran.

IPB READING LIST

ICE PLANET BARBARIANS

Ice Planet Barbarians

Barbarian Alien

Barbarian Lover

Barbarian Mine

Ice Planet Holiday (novella)

Barbarian's Prize

Barbarian's Mate

Having the Barbarian's Baby (short story)

Ice Ice Babies (short story)

Barbarian's Touch

Calm(short story)

Barbarian's Taming

Aftershocks (short story)

Barbarian's Heart

Barbarian's Hope

Barbarian's Choice

Barbarian's Redemption

Barbarian's Lady

ALSO BY RUBY DIXON

FIREBLOOD DRAGONS

Fire in His Blood

Fire in His Kiss

Fire in His Embrace

Fire in His Fury

Fire In His Spirit

Fire in His Veins

ICEHOME

LAUREN'S BARBARIAN

VERONICA'S DRAGON

WILLA'S BEAST

GAIL'S FAMILY

ANGIE'S GLADIATOR

CORSAIRS

THE CORSAIR'S CAPTIVE

IN THE CORSAIR'S BED

ENTICED BY THE CORSAIR

DECEIVING THE CORSAIR

STAND ALONE

PRISON PLANET BARBARIAN

THE ALIEN'S MAIL-ORDER BRIDE

BEAUTY IN AUTUMN

THE KING'S SPINSTER BRIDE

THE ALIEN ASSASSIN'S CONVENIENT WIFE

BEDLAM BUTCHERS

Bedlam Butchers, Volumes 1-3: Off Limits, Packing Double, Double Trouble

Bedlam Butchers, Volumes 4-6: Double Down, Double or Nothing, Slow Ride

Double Dare You

BEAR BITES

SHIFT: Five Complete Novellas

WANT MORE?

For more information about upcoming books in the Ice Planet Barbarians, Fireblood Dragons, or any other books by Ruby Dixon, like me on Facebook or subscribe to my new release newsletter. I love sharing snippets of books in progress and fan art! Come join the fun.

As always - thanks for reading!

<3 Ruby

PS - Want to discuss my books without me staring over your shoulder? There's a group for that, too! Ruby Dixon - Blue Barbarian Babes (over on Facebook) has all of your barbarian and dragon needs. :) Enjoy!

PPS - I'm now on Instagram!

Made in the USA
Coppell, TX
28 August 2023